# BRAVE

# A FRACTURED FAIRY TALE

By

J.E. Taylor

Brave:A Fractured Fairy Tale ©
January 2023 J.E. Taylor

**An ultimatum. A curse. A forbidden love.**

May Stewart's father, King James VII, demands she choose a husband within a fortnight. The list of approved suitors leaves her uninspired at the courtship festivities until fate intervenes, and an uninvited stranger sparks her interest.

Unfortunately, even uttering handsome Aiden MacMahon's surname is a capital offense, for it whispers of a dark curse that dictates the daylight belongs to the beast on their family crest.

The MacMahon name is *not* a choice the king will allow for May, but she cannot deny the connection she has with Aiden.

When May discovers her own secret lineage holds the key to reversing the MacMahon curse, her choice of suitor becomes so much more than just a marriage match.

But choosing Aiden MacMahon could lead them both into death's icy embrace.

# BRAVE Chapter 1

BEING BRANDED WITH A hot iron would be a more pleasant experience than this fresh hell.

My gaze rose to the ornate architecture surrounding the throne room as the last in the long line of suitors bumbled through his offer for my hand. My father, King James Stewart VII, sat on the throne with my mother next to him. He played with his white-speckled beard while his gaze remained stoic. It was one of his more identifiable tells. He was just as bored with these simpering fools as I was. My mother, on the other hand, seemed to be enthralled with each suitor. She smiled endlessly and every so often she wound a stray wisp of her auburn hair around her finger as she listened.

She was trying, which was more than I could say for me. My father called these men noble, but while they may have been from a family with high political or social ties, they certainly did not represent what noble meant to me. This entire ordeal was a farce, and what made things worse was my father expected me to pick a husband from this sad lot.

It wasn't as if they were the bane of human existence—a couple of them were lookers—but none of them truly had what I was looking for. Spark. Fire. Passion. These things were missing, replaced with a cockiness that I abhorred. Their demeanor suggested I should be the one bowing down to them, as if God had granted me a unique viewing of perfection incarnate. Others offered the brawn without the brains, and I really needed someone intellectually stimulating.

I glanced at my father after the last had stated his lineage and what he offered. Every one of them only offered goods in exchange for my hand, like I was something to barter for instead of an equal to build a lasting connection with.

If one had said he offered a promise of a lifetime of adventure, love, and happiness, that would have been the man I chose in a heartbeat. I wanted someone who saw me as their partner, not a possession.

Not one of these men would do. I met my father's gaze and shook my head.

He gave a wave, and the room cleared. Both my parents waited until the audience was gone and the doors to the throne room closed before turning to me.

"May, what was wrong with these men?" my father asked.

My mother let out a chuckle and exchanged a glance with me. "They think of her as a prize, sweetheart. Not a heart to be won."

"That's poppycock and you know it," he said as he stood.

"Did you hear a one offering her a future like no other?" she asked.

My father's lips thinned. "This isn't negotiable. You are going to choose a suitor, one whom I approve of, within the next fortnight. Understand?"

"Do you not want your only daughter to be as happy as we are?" my mother chided.

"My dear, Katherine," he said, taking my mother's hands, "our marriage was arranged as well."

"Aye, but I did not know that when you went about wooing me. You had long weaseled your way into my heart before my parents told me we were already betrothed. Had you come before me in this setting, in the way these boys did, I would have scoffed just as much as May."

I could see the wheels in my father's head plotting against me with his choice of a proper husband. "I will choose when I am good and ready," I said.

"You have a fortnight. If not, I will choose for you." He gave me a final nod before he spun and stalked out of the throne room.

My mother sighed and turned her gaze to me. "You're going to have to stop being so fussy, my dear." She glanced at the window as the last of the light faded from the sky. "It's time to gather in the great hall."

I sighed and brushed my flame-red hair out of my face. "Do I have to?"

"Aye. Mingle, see if anyone grows on you."

"Fine." I followed her to the great hall where the families of the line of men volleying for my attentions all gathered.

The tension in the room was as thick as the scent of the feast. The boys posturing with each other was like watching dueling roosters. The minute they noticed I was in the room, they made a mad dash to my side, doting on me in the most annoying of ways.

While most girls would love a group of men getting her drinks, and food, and dessert, nearly falling all over themselves to do so, it grated on my nerves.

"I can feed myself," I snapped as spoons and forks were shoved in my face. "Now, please, give me some space!"

As if they were one single unit, they all stepped back, letting me breathe a little before they all tried to engage in further conversation.

That was when *he* caught my eye.

A man stood in the shadows, leaning against the wall in a manner that was both relaxed and possibly the sexiest damn thing I had ever seen. He had not been amongst the suitors in the throne room. I would have remembered that intense stare and sense of aloofness.

He stood taller than most men in the room with a build that was one hundred percent muscle filling out his shirt and his tight knickers. His dark hair curled at the ends, matching the lashes on his bedroom eyes, the blue of his irises as distinctly bright as the daytime sky.

He kept my gaze, and a hint of a dimple appeared in his cheek before he gave me a slow nod of acknowledgement.

I wondered if he had the mind to go with all that eye candy. Curiosity won out, and I crossed the room. All talk ceased when I stopped a few feet from the interesting stranger, studying him. Up close, he was even more stunning than from a distance, especially when he flashed a smile revealing a set of the whitest teeth I had seen all day.

"Princess May," he said in a deep baritone voice that dried all the saliva in my mouth. He bowed with the formality of common folk, but his clothes indicated he came from the highborn class.

"I am at a disadvantage. You know my name, but I have yet to make your acquaintance." I couldn't help continuing my study of the man. I had to staunch the urge to reach out and touch his chest to settle the silent argument in my head that he was just a figment of my imagination.

"Aidan MacMahon," he said.

"Aidan." The name played on my tongue in the most delicious manner.

He cleared his throat and grinned as his eyes panned the audience behind me. "I apologize for missing the formalities in the throne room." An interesting hue of pink bloomed in his cheeks, and his gaze dropped to mine again. "But I could not make it in time."

A litany of questions came to mind, but I didn't know which one to ask first, so instead, I bit my bottom lip and just stared into the depth of his eyes. Being tongue-tied wasn't my usual affliction, but Aidan seemed to have that effect on me. He didn't seem to mind the silence between us. In fact, it almost suited him.

I blinked, broke eye contact, and licked my lips. "May I inquire as to why you missed the formalities?"

He laughed lightly. "I had a bear of a time getting here." He winked at me, and then his gaze moved over my head. He dropped to his knee. "Your Highness," he said and bowed his head.

My father stepped by my side with narrowed eyes. "You were not among the nobles in the throne room," he said with a sharpness that made me want to cower.

"No, Your Highness. My duties required my attention. Therefore, I was unable to make it in time." Aidan stood, but kept his eyes averted.

My father crossed his arms, unimpressed by Aidan's response. "Are you of noble blood, boy?"

Aidan's gaze jumped to my father's and then mine. He shifted his weight and nodded. "Aye, but it is an ancient line that has all but been forgotten."

"And what line might that be?"

Aidan sighed and cleared his throat. "The House of MacMahon." His voice was so soft it was almost a whisper that only my father and I could pick up in the din.

My father tilted his head and narrowed his eyes. "Didn't they die off nearly a hundred years ago?"

Aidan shrugged. "Almost, but not all of us were put down."

The way he described his family's demise piqued my interest. The phrase "put down" was usually reserved for animals, not human beings. His gaze moved from my father's to mine, and it set a fire in my soul.

"I suggest you find your way out. Now." My father gripped my arm and turned, leading me away from Aidan.

I glanced over my shoulder and caught Aidan's frown. His shoulders sagged, and he turned, disappearing into the dark hallway.

My heart dropped into my stomach. I sent a glare at my father. "Why did you do that?"

"Because the MacMahons are cursed."

I stopped walking. "Explain," I demanded.

"No. You have a fortnight. I suggest you find a proper suitor among the men who are here."

"And if I said I choose Aiden MacMahon?" The words slipped out of my mouth before I could catch them. Being obstinate was a part of my charm, but my father did not take it well.

He paled and pressed his lips together. "That is not an option." He let go of my arm and sauntered away.

The moment he left my side, the vultures attacked as adamantly as they had before. Each boy vied for my attention, but my mind was elsewhere. I half listened to their stories, nodding occasionally until I finally excused myself.

I could not take their leering any longer.

As I walked away, a fight broke out between a few of the boys. I did not stop to see what the outcome was. I had no interest in any of them. The only man tonight who sparked my curiosity was forbidden.

# BRAVE Chapter 2

THE CASTLE CLEARED OUT by the middle of the next day. I made my way to the grand hall to get some food, happy with the quiet now permeating the building. It gave me a chance to really focus on all that had transpired the prior evening.

In the wee hours of the night, I had made up my mind. Aiden MacMahon was at the top of my list. Curse be damned. If my father wouldn't agree to the arrangement, then I would refuse to marry any suitor he chose. I knew my position would incite the full fury of my father, but he'd clearly stated I needed to make a choice, and soon.

My parents looked up as I entered the dining hall. My father sat back in the chair and crossed his arms. "I have narrowed the field down to the House of Cameron, House of Dundas, and House of Fergusson." His tone was magnanimous, as if the men who had those affiliations were the only ones on Earth.

They were the ones who had offered the most for my hand. I ground my teeth together. My hands clenched, and I shook my head. "No."

His eyebrows shot up in surprise, and my mother looked up from her stitchery.

"MacMahon," I said.

My mother gasped as if I'd said a forbidden word. She covered her mouth, and her eyes widened like a frightened child's. "You cannot utter that name, ever!"

"Why not?"

"Because it is a capital offence to bear that name," my father said, glaring at me. "That is what I meant by the family is cursed. The fact that the young man stated his house in the confines of my castle means he is daft, or actively looking for death." He pulled out a parchment from his pocket and handed it to me.

I unrolled the thin paper and read the words of a king who had ruled the lands in the early years. He denounced the surname MacMahon and promised death to all who still claimed the name. I stared at the law and shivered before I threw the roll back at my father.

"You are the king, and you can withdraw this ludicrous decree."

His face reddened.

I turned on my heel and left the room before either of them could say a word. My stomach rumbled, but it was nothing compared to the rage pumping heat through my veins.

Why on God's green earth would a king wipe out an entire house and set forth such a vile order?

My stomach growled as the lessons I was taught of our history came flooding back. The name and all its gory history came forth. Their clan had attacked the king, along with the noble class, in a futile effort to overtake the throne. Thus, the law. My belly churned, demanding food, so I grabbed my bow and a full quiver of arrows and headed out of the castle. On foot, I stormed into the woods, hellbent on finding my own sustenance.

Muttering under my breath and walking with a heavy foot paid a warning to all woodland animals. I took a deep breath, closing my eyes and calming the burn in my chest. With my anger under control, I opened my eyes and readied my bow.

I walked with a lighter step, near silent in my quest. Deeper into the forest, I went until the sunlight faded in the thick canopy above. I had no sense in how far I had traveled from home, but I was intent on catching a rabbit or a squirrel.

I approached a grove of thick trees and dense brush. There didn't seem to be an obvious way through. My arms dropped to my sides as I searched for a reasonable way around the obstruction. A rumble built behind me, like a roll of thunder. I spun, bringing my arrow back to my bow.

A large brown bear stood behind me, but his eyes were not normal brown. No, they were as blue as the late afternoon sky peeking through the leaves above. His feral growl ceased the moment I faced him, and he dropped to all fours with a huff that disturbed the strands of my hair.

My heart slammed in my chest. My hands shook as I stared at the beast down the shaft of my arrow. He was just as frozen to the spot as I was, our eyes locked in some strange death dare. And then he turned and lumbered through the woods at a speed that I never would have imagined a beast that big could attain.

Instead of firing my arrow, I ran after the bear, pulled along by something stronger than my curiosity. It was then I realized the darkness falling on the woods had nothing to do with the canopy above. My senses cleared as I stepped into a field. The bear galloped across the open space as the last of the sun's rays faded.

I followed. Before the bear reached the woods on the far side, he reared up on his legs. I slid to a stop as light surrounded the animal. It roared as the glow transformed it. When the glare died down, the beast was now a man.

My eyes widened at the naked male a hundred yards away. He stretched, making every muscle glisten as it flexed. When he turned in my direction, I gasped at the familiar profile. His eyes widened as well.

We stood frozen in time, our gazes locked together in a mesmerizing dance of shock and recognition. He looked away, breaking whatever hold he had over me. When he turned and headed for the woods, my feet moved from the spot I stood.

"Aiden, wait!" I called as I sprinted towards him.

He stopped, keeping his back towards me.

I slowed as I approached. My eyes kept wandering down to his muscular ass. I had to stifle the urge to reach out and cup it just to see if it was as firm as it looked under the moonlight.

"What are you doing out this far from the castle, Princess?"

His gruff tone made all the hairs on my neck stand on end. "I was looking for some food, and I didn't realize it had gotten so late."

"Don't they have enough food in the castle?" He glared over his shoulder at me.

I sucked in my bottom lip and nodded. "I just didn't want to share a meal with my father."

He nodded and stepped towards the woods.

"Where are you going?"

"To get a pair of pants on, if you don't mind," he said without looking over his shoulder. "Just wait here. I'll be back in a moment, and then I will make sure you get back to the castle safely."

He disappeared into the woods and came back a few minutes later dressed in pants, boots, and a half-buttoned shirt. As disappointed as I was that he had covered his nakedness, I had to admit how good he looked in his rugged clothes.

"My father thinks you are either daft or have a death wish," I said as he approached.

A dimple appeared in his cheek. "What say you on the matter?"

"I haven't the foggiest idea. I am still trying to reconcile the bear with the man." I waved the arrow in his direction and then slid it back into my quiver. I shouldered my bow and cocked my head at him. "My father also said you come from a cursed clan."

Aiden laughed, and the rich sound of it tickled my fancy. "Did your father also tell you who cursed our family?"

I shook my head and followed him as he stepped onto a beaten path in the woods.

"His ancestors had a witch at their disposal and not only did they mark the MacMahon name forevermore, they had that witch curse the entire lineage. I have yet to see the sun rise or set. I am cursed to bear the symbol of our name during the daylight and wander as a man while the moon crosses the sky. This is why I did not make it to the throne room in time, and I suspect it is why the king never has evening viewings, so I cannot challenge his authority."

Venom filled his voice, and his glare caused shivers across my skin. I slowed, putting a little distance between us.

He stopped and turned towards me. "You are afraid?"

My heartbeat thrummed in my ears, but I wasn't willing to admit I was afraid. I shook my head.

He stepped closer and leaned in, inhaling through flared nostrils. "Your scent says otherwise."

I pressed my lips together against the nervous energy in my stomach. "Well, can you blame me?" I had seen a lot of strange, unexplained things in my twenty years on this earth, but seeing a bear turn into a man, sexy or otherwise, had me a little scatterbrained. Especially one who blamed my family for his dire circumstances. "How do I know you are not leading me deep into the woods where you plan on eating me?"

He stared down at me with a wicked grin. The light dancing in his eyes matched the salaciousness of his smile. "There's an idea," he whispered with a sexy growl, and pulled me against his hard body. "But I'm sure if I did something so sinful, you would have my head on a platter."

I blinked at him as his words sank in. He wasn't talking about having me for dinner. Heat filled my entire form, exploding in my cheeks as I pushed him away.

"If you had stood in front of my father yesterday, what is it you would have said?" I asked, changing the subject. I walked on the path, letting him follow me this time.

He didn't answer me right away. Instead, he walked at my side with his thumbs latched on the edge of his pockets. A crease appeared between his eyes as if in deep thought.

"Whatever I had the mind to say changed the minute I laid eyes on you." He sighed and glanced sideways at me.

"How so?"

"One does not challenge the king to a duel for the right to keep his name on the eve where the king's only daughter is to claim her life partner. Especially when the sight of her melts all one's resolve, replacing it with a need so strong that namesake or curses no longer matter."

I digested his words. "So, you do have a death wish," I said, meeting his intense gaze.

He stopped and cocked his head, narrowing his eyes at me. The flare of red in his cheeks preceded his swagger down the path in front of me.

A smirk toyed on my lips, and any fear that had been at the edges of my mind dispersed. Aiden had felt the connection as acutely as I had the prior evening. And he did not refer to my dilemma as having to choose a prince or a betrothal. He'd said the magic word. Partner.

I slammed into his back.

"What..."

He partially turned with his finger on his lips, telling me to shush.

I didn't move. He smelled of honey and the deep woods. I closed my eyes, getting lost in his unique scent.

"Hand me your bow and an arrow, quietly," he whispered.

I placed the bow in his waiting hand, pulled an arrow out of my quiver, and handed it to him over his shoulder. The woods were too dark to see what had him spooked.

"Please have another arrow ready once this one flies," he said and pulled the bow back.

A low rumbling growl came from the blackness in front of us, and it took me a moment to place that sound. Aiden exhaled, and the twang of the bow as he let the arrow go drowned out the growls. Before he ripped the next arrow from my hand, a howl of pain filled the darkness.

He let the second arrow fly. "Another!"

The urgency in his voice sparked me into action. The moment I slammed the arrow into the palm of his hand, another pain-filled howl sounded. Moments after the third arrow took flight, that same high-pitched whine shocked my ears.

"They are getting much bolder these days," Aiden muttered under his breath as he handed me the bow and sauntered off into the darkness.

By the time I caught up to him, he had three scrawny wolves hauled over his shoulder and a small pup held by the scruff of its neck in front of him.

"Don't hurt it," I said, hurrying to his side. I reached for the wolf pup.

Aiden hesitantly handed it over. The little thing mewed in my arms, crying for a mother that was now just a wolf pelt over Aiden's shoulder.

"If they had stayed in the shadows and left us alone, that pup might still have a mother." He started walking again and glanced over his shoulder. "What are you going to do with that thing?"

"I'm going to keep him and name him…Shadow."

"Are you sure that is going to fly with mommy and daddy?" he asked, mocking my exuberance over the small life I held in my arms.

"Well, considering I haven't planted an arrow in your heart like the law states I should, I wouldn't worry too much about what my parents think about a wolf pup. I would worry more about what they will do to you if you show your face in the castle again."

He slowed and kept pace next to me.

I glanced at him. "What would you have offered my father for my hand?"

He chuckled. "I have nothing of monetary value to offer, Princess. Besides, bartering for a lady's hand is an archaic practice. A heart should be won, not traded for goods."

It was as if this man had been inside my head.

We walked in silence, the wolf pup cradled in my arms, sleeping peacefully. Aiden held the bow loosely in one hand and had his other wrapped around the three wolves hanging over his shoulder. Carrying three adult wolves did not seem to be a burden to Aiden. My heart fluttered as I watched his easy stride.

There had to be a way to convince my father that Aiden MacMahon was the right man for me.

# BRAVE Chapter 3

"WHO GOES THERE?" A guard at the gate asked as we approached.

"Tis I, Princess May," I answered, taking the position in front of Aiden. "Stay close," I whispered over my shoulder.

"The king has been looking for you." He raised the gate for us to enter and gave Aiden a sideways glance.

"This nice gentleman found me in the woods and helped me find my way back." I kept going as if all was normal.

It was a gamble bringing Aiden into the castle, especially with all that had transpired in the last twenty-four hours, but I needed to show my father that the law was ludicrous. Only he had the power to change it.

As for the curse, I would have to look into that further once things settled down. My mind was made up. I would do whatever it took to make sure Aiden was pardoned for the sins of his ancestors and reverse the damn curse that turned him into a beast by day.

"Stop that man!"

I jumped at the sound of my father's voice. We were halfway across the courtyard, and guards came out of the woodwork, all brandishing swords.

Aiden handed me my bow and laid the wolves on the ground before him. He raised his hands, showing he would not fight. The guardsmen, however, approached as if he were fully armed for battle.

I stepped close to Aiden out of a need to protect him. "He saved me from these wolves." I pointed to the pile on the ground. "And spared the pup in my arms. He is not a danger."

"He is a MacMahon," my father growled, stepping into the moonlight. "And as such, is sentenced to death."

"Is there no mercy for the man who saved your daughter's life? A man who insisted on accompanying me to safety without so much as a thought for his own?"

My father's lips pressed together, and his hands clenched into fists. The way his face pinched, I knew my words were puncturing his resolve.

"The law of the land…" he started.

"*Can* be changed," I interjected. "He is not his ancestors. He is not the ones who terrorized the nobles and stormed the castle over a hundred years ago. Why should he be crucified for his ancestor's sins?" I stood my ground, challenging my father in front of his guardsmen. My palms sweat under the heat of the puppy still in my arms. My stomach clenched at my audacity, and nerves bit at the surface of my skin. My heart pounded as I prayed I had not just taken away any chance for Aidan's survival.

"May, this is my battle, not yours," Aiden said softly.

I glanced at him and swallowed the lump in my throat.

"Take him to the dungeon," my father growled, glaring at me in a way that promised an epic lecture about his dignity in front of his men.

The order was a concession, but it didn't mean Aiden was out of danger.

"Don't hurt him," I said as the guards grabbed Aiden and shoved him forward. They were not known for their patience or their gentleness with prisoners, and while I knew Aiden would live until my father saw fit to pass his sentence, I didn't know if it would be without bruises or broken bones.

As soon as Aiden was out of sight, my father stormed over to where I stood. He glanced down at the dead wolves and then the puppy in my arms. His jaw clenched tight and his glare was as deadly as I had ever seen it.

"I should lock you up in your room until your wedding day."

"You are the one who dictated I make a choice." I glared back at him. My voice was low and full of the same venom his words held. "And if you see fit to execute Aiden, I will never agree to marry anyone you decide is worthy. If you try to force it on me, you will not like my reaction."

"Do not threaten me, girl." He stepped closer, towering over me.

"It's not a threat, Father. It is a promise."

A small growl came from my arms. The little wolf pup was about as pleased with my father as I was. I scratched behind the wolf's ear and the growl faded, but its sharp little eyes never left my father.

"I should have beaten this obstinance out of you the first time you showed it."

"Mother wouldn't have allowed that."

He pressed his lips together. "Go to your room. Now."

Instead of instigating him further, I turned and trudged inside with Shadow still in my arms. My father ordered someone to bring him the pelts of the wolves once they were cleaned, and I shuddered, clasping my wolf pup a little tighter.

"Sheri, can you please get me a bowl of milk?" I asked my lady-in-waiting as I entered my room.

"Right away, my lady." She scuttled out of the room and returned with a bowl of milk a few minutes later.

I took the milk and put it under Shadow's nose. The pup nearly dove into the bowl. Both paws and his snout dipped into the white liquid as if it were made of gold. His tongue lapped the liquid as fast as possible, splattering it all over the front of his fine gray coat. I smiled at my little treasure.

But my smile disappeared as my mother stormed into my bedroom, her face as red as her hair.

She stopped halfway across the room, planting her hands on her hips as she stared down at me. "What have you done?"

My eyebrows rose in response and the little ball of fur in my lap started that low growl. The hair on the back of Shadow's neck bristled. I slowly ran my fingers down behind his ears, scratching to distract him. My mother wasn't one to take being challenged lightly, and the sternness in her expression matched that of her demanding tone.

She turned and started pacing the length of the room. Red bloomed in her cheeks, and she chewed on her lower lip.

"Why are you so upset?" I finally asked when the pacing didn't cease.

She stopped and turned, facing me. "Bringing him here was not wise," she finally said, with eyes so full of fear that I gulped whatever words had been waiting to come out.

"Shadow?" I asked, holding my wolf a little tighter.

My mother rolled her eyes. "No. MacMahon."

"He wasn't willing to let me cross the fields alone. Not after the wolves attacked us in the woods."

"You should have insisted!"

I leaned back away from the panic pulsing out of my mother. "Why?"

"Because..." She clamped her lips closed and shut her eyes. When she opened them, I swore there were unshed tears before she blinked them away. "Because he wants your blood."

I cocked my head. "If he wanted my blood, why in the world wouldn't he have taken it in the forest?" Her logic did not sit right with him protecting me the way he'd done. "He had plenty of opportunity to kill me, Mother. And he did just the opposite. He protected me."

"Of course he protected you. If you die, the curse becomes permanent."

I stared at her, trying to comprehend what exactly she was telling me. "What?" The word came out in barely a whisper.

"You are his key to reversing the curse, but if you die before the ritual is complete, he will become the bear for all time."

"How am I the key?"

She bit her lower lip again. "You are the only female descendent of the witch who placed the curse on the MacMahons. That is why that heathen came to the palace."

"I still don't understand how I am the key." I ignored the fact I was a descendent of a witch. I would deal with that once I understood how I factored into Aiden's cure.

"In order to reverse the curse, the last descendant of the MacMahon clan must drink a qist of fresh blood from the last descendant of the witch Marigold within the confines of the great stones when the mid-day hour becomes as dark as night. If Marigold's descendant lives despite the loss of blood, it will cure the curse. But if Marigold's descendant dies before the sun takes over the sky once again, then the last MacMahon will die with her, and only the beast will remain."

My mind raced just as fast as my heart. "So, my blood and being at Stonehenge during an eclipse will cure Aiden?"

My mother paled and reached for the bedside table to steady herself. Her slow nod of acknowledgement created a pressure inside my chest.

"What if the last descendant of Marigold and MacMahon were to wed?"

"It is forbidden." She looked at the pup in my lap. "Just as it is forbidden to have wolves as pets."

I cocked an eyebrow at her. "Shadow isn't going anywhere." I bit my tongue before I added anything about Aiden. I had to have a conversation with the man before I stuck my neck out for him again.

Had his attentions all been a ruse?

LONG AFTER THE CASTLE quieted, I slipped out of my room and down to the dungeons, sneaking by the dozing watch guard. I snatched the keys off the table next to him. As stealthily as possible, I tried each key in the door to the vault until the click of the lock echoed. I stiffened.

The guard mumbled and shifted, but didn't wake. Finally, I exhaled the breath I had been holding and slipped through the door, closing it behind me. I lit the lantern and kept it on low as I tiptoed down the hall, glancing into each cell.

I stopped when the light shone on Aiden.

"Why have you come?" Aiden asked from his prone position on the bare cot. He didn't even lift his head to look at me.

"I was going to ask you the same thing." I turned up the lantern and glanced at the door to the castle proper. If the guard woke, I would be in a great deal of trouble. I inspected the keys in my hand until I found one that looked like the lock on the door, slid the metal inside, and turned it. At first it didn't budge, but a moment later, a satisfying click sounded. I opened the door and stood at the entrance to the cell.

His eyes opened, and he sat up, meeting my gaze. A dimple appeared quick before it disappeared. "I have a dilemma," he said and sighed, glancing down at the floor. "I want a whole life." He stood and crossed to the bars. Fire burned in his eyes, and the next few words came out between clenched teeth. "I wanted it bad enough to believe the sacrifice was worth it."

His intense stare froze me in place. When his hand snaked out and tangled in my hair, his touch zapped me with enough sizzle to create steam between us. He pulled me closer. The metal of the lamp handle bit into my hand as I gripped it tighter, and my breath caught in my throat.

"And then I saw you." He leaned his head against mine. His dark bangs tickled my forehead as his thumb caressed my cheek. "That was as bad as a kick in the balls."

"Why?" My voice barely registered.

He met my gaze, and it was as if the room had ignited. His lips covered mine as he swung me around and pressed me against the bars. I gasped. His tongue slipped into my mouth in a delicious dance, exploring, twirling, teasing. One of his hands caressed my breast through my nightshirt before he pulled away.

"What I wouldn't do to hear you calling my name in ecstasy..." His lips touched mine, and then he was gone.

The cell clanged shut, leaving me in the grungy accommodations as he slipped out the door.

He glanced over his shoulder before he disappeared into the dark, like a soldier looking at his loved ones just before he was shipped off to battle.

"Damn you," I muttered under my breath and pushed on the gate. It didn't budge. I hadn't even noticed him taking the lamp or the keys out of my grasp. I was too lost in the sweetness of his mouth and the gentleness of his hand cupping my breast.

I pressed my lips together against a scream of frustration. Alerting the guards would be an immediate death sentence for Aiden. I was angry with him, but not enough to put his life at risk.

I sat down on the cot, letting out a huff. A waft of Aiden's sweet honey scent drifted from the thin fabric, and I closed my eyes, allowing myself a moment to relish his smell. It dissipated as quickly as Aiden had. I ground my teeth together, lying back on the lumpy fabric while I waited for someone to uncover my duplicity.

# BRAVE Chapter 4

SHADOW'S DISTANT HOWL PULLED me from a restless sleep. I sat up on the cot and rubbed my eyes, letting them adjust to the dank cell. The morning sunrise lit up the space.

I certainly hoped Aiden made it out of the castle, because no one inside these walls would spare the life of a wild bear.

The howling ended. My heart jumped into my throat. Had someone cut my wolf down? Tears stung my eyes.

The door at the end of the hall opened and light from a lamp illuminated the hall outside my cell. The sleek form of Shadow stopped in front of the cell and whined. When my father stepped next to him, the stoic expression on his face made me gulp.

His gaze traveled over the entire cell before it landed back on me. His lips pressed into a thin line, and the red hue filling his cheeks and nose announced his aggravation as loud as a crack of thunder in a stormy sky.

"Where is he?" he asked in a menacing growl that made me glad a row of bars stood between us.

I shrugged. "Probably halfway across the country by now."

He closed his eyes and his nostrils flared.

I bit my lip, waiting for my punishment to be delivered. But my father just turned and sauntered down the hallway, leaving Shadow and me alone in the dungeon.

My wolf pup stretched out on the floor outside the cell and put his head on his paws. His sigh filled the stale air. I flopped down on the cot again and stared at the ceiling as the morning light shined brighter through the window.

I didn't know how much time passed, but the room was at its brightest when Sheri snuck into the dungeon with a plate of food for me and a bowl of milk for Shadow. I nearly attacked the food through the bars. It had been over twenty-four hours since I'd had a proper meal.

"I had to sneak by the old guard to bring this to you. Your father ordered that no one was to come in here," she whispered.

"Thank you," I said after I stuffed the last morsel into my mouth.

Sheri smiled, reached down, and picked up Shadow's empty bowl.

Her words sank in. "Old guard?" The only time father put elderly guards to work was when he and the rest of his army were out of the castle.

Sheri nodded. "Aye. The king called his army together to go bear hunting."

My heart nearly stopped in my chest, and I gripped the bars. "Get me out of here."

She stepped away from the bars, her eyes wide with fear. "I can't. Your father threatened me. Told me that if I helped you, he would have my head on the post outside the castle." Sheri hurried out of the dungeon.

I banged my forehead against the bars and let out a yell of frustration. The echo in the empty dungeon ran a cold shiver up my spine. I gritted my teeth and closed my eyes, holding on to the bars until my knuckles ached. Fury and fear played in my bloodstream, making every fiber hum.

I released my grip on the cold iron and stepped back. I tilted my head to the ceiling and bellowed every ounce of anger in an ethereal cry.

The guard rushed into the cell and slid to a stop in front of my cage. His chest rose and fell in frantic gasps as he stared at me with wide eyes.

"Let me out," I growled, sounding as feral as those wolves had last night.

He fumbled with the keys and dropped them on the floor before reclaiming them with shaking hands. He slid the key in the lock and threw the door open, then plastered himself against the wall on the far side of the hallway.

I stepped out of the cage and put my hand out. "Your sword," I demanded.

He blinked and then undid his belt, handing it over to me with the sword still in its scabbard. I clasped the leather around my waist and stormed out of the dungeon with Shadow on my heels. Instead of exiting the castle through the courtyard where I would surely have been caught and detained, I went out the secret path that led to the woods on the far side of the castle.

I had no idea where I was headed, but an internal guide pulled me along until I stood just outside the forest, staring at Stonehenge. My chest constricted at the sight of my father's army closing in on the stones from all sides. I ran, unsheathing my sword. Shadow kept pace with me as we raced across the field. I weaved through the line, sliding under the arms that reached to grab me and broke free of the group, rounding the entry until I stood alone in the center of the great stones.

I turned in a circle as the rumble of footsteps outside the walls pounded up my legs. I stopped my inspection at the sight of the bear in the far corner, cowering away from the sound. His back and sides were protected by the rocks.

Shadow and I approached, bent on blocking the only way to get to him. His gaze moved in my direction now that I'd shifted position into a downwind draft. His eyes widened, and he backed into the rocks more.

I turned, thinking the guards had breached the rocks. No one had entered. With my heart beating so hard that the whoosh of blood in my ears drowned out the sound, I turned back to the bear. Forcing my breathing to slow, I sheathed the sword and put my hands out to show him I was unarmed.

The beast's reaction didn't change. I glanced down at Shadow and he was looking up at me with his head cocked, like he was waiting for his next instructions. His gaze jumped behind me, and I turned, pulling the sword out, putting myself between my father's army and the bear.

I held the sword at the ready, lightly bouncing on the balls of my feet. The guards parted, and my father stepped through the line.

A deep crease appeared between his eyes. "May?" His gaze traveled down my body and then back to my face.

I looked down at my thin nightshirt. The belt held my bodice tight against my breasts, and my legs were bare from just above the knee.

The men surrounding him shifted uncomfortably as they attempted to avert their eyes from so much bare flesh.

None of them were in battle-ready stances, but that did not sway me from keeping vigilant.

"Move out of the way," my father said, recovering from his prior shock.

"I'm sorry, Father. I cannot let you or any of your men pass." My voice was calm, despite my racing heart and dry mouth. There were too many of them. If they all charged at once, I wouldn't stand a chance. But I was the king's daughter and rightful heir to the throne.

His hands clenched, and his sharp glare sent a shiver over my bare skin.

"Leave us. Go back to the castle," he commanded.

The army filtered out, leaving only my father and me with Shadow and the bear in the clearing.

The moment we were alone, he unsheathed his sword and pointed it at me. "You really want to play this out?"

I took the stance he'd taught me. "When I win, you will pardon Aiden." I had never bested my father in a sword fight. Hell, we'd never fought with real steel before, and I wasn't as sure of myself as I projected.

He stepped forward, and so did I. Shadow moved between us, growling in an effort to protect me.

"Oh, for Heaven's sake," my father said and lowered his sword as he stared at Shadow.

I used the diversion to my advantage and swung my sword. It was met with steel; the impact vibrating all the way up my arms. My father sneered.

The bear behind us roared. We both turned to see the thing rear up on its hind legs. It was then that its dark eyes struck me. Aiden's eyes were blue, not brown like this beast.

I gasped and pushed backwards into my father's chest. "That's not Aiden."

"How do you know?" my father asked, moving, so he was at my side.

"Because Aiden's eyes are blue, even when he is in bear form."

We both readied our swords, moving away from each other, strategically splitting the bear's focus. How I wished my father hadn't sent the army away. We could use a little back up right now.

Shadow continued to growl, but this time his attentions were on the bear and not my father and me.

"Shadow, come here!" I snapped, and the wolf pup obediently took up residence at my side.

The bear thundered at us, its head swinging from side to side, trying to keep both of us in view as he stepped closer. His massive paw swatted in my direction. I dropped to the ground, grasping my sword with all my strength. The tip caught its paw, and the power of his swing knocked the handle right out of my grip. I rolled in the opposite direction from my sword, trying to put distance between me and the furious animal.

"Hey!" my father yelled, calling the bear's attention away from me.

Blood dripped from the paw I'd sliced, and the beast swung it at my father. My father wasn't as quick as I had been, and the bear's claws caught his breastplate, flinging him against the rocks.

My father slumped to the ground.

The bear went after him.

"No!" I yelled.

It spun toward me.

Shadow growled. All the hair on the back of his neck stood on end. My little wolf pup was no match for an adult bear, and neither was I.

I scooped Shadow up in my arms and backed away, trying to draw the bear away from my father. My heart slammed against the walls of my chest as I calculated my dwindling odds.

My sword was too far away, and my father was just coming to in the far corner. Blood flowed down his face, and he rose on shaking legs.

The bear lumbered towards Shadow's fearless growl. I backed into a rock, staring down the snarling bear.

He cocked his giant paw back, ready to swipe his sharp claws from my crown to my toes.

A brown blur flew through the air and hit the grizzly before he could strike his death blow. The ball of fur rolled away in a pile of roars and howls of pain.

Blue eyes amidst brown fur flashed before another blow knocked him back. The fight raged, leaving me shaking and cowering behind my little rock fort.

My father hid behind a boulder as well, and I caught his eye. He tilted his head towards the fighting bears. I nodded. He needed to know it was Aiden who had saved me yet again from a horrible fate.

The slam of bone meeting rock echoed. One bear went down hard. The remaining bear fell onto all fours and turned towards me, snarling, his brown eyes full of fury.

"No!" I dropped Shadow to the ground, sprinting to where my sword lay. Hot anguish and rage fueled every cell, and I slid, swiping my blade from the ground and bouncing to my feet. I spun towards the beast, holding the blade like a javelin.

The grizzly reared up with a roar. My scream matched his.

I launched the blade at the same moment my father appeared in the air behind the bear with his blade clasped in two hands over his head. The bear was not fast enough to knock my sword off target. It buried in his chest all the way to the hilt. My father's blade sank into the base of the beast's neck. Bone was no match for the metal and the snap of it resounded.

The bear took a shaky step towards me and then collapsed. I spun out of the way and when he hit the ground; it shook like a mighty earthquake.

My father stood behind the dead bear, looking more formidable than I had ever seen him. He gave me a nod of approval, even though his chest heaved from exertion.

My gaze fell to my blue-eyed bear, and I ran to where he lay. Shadow followed, whining as he sniffed the prone animal. He lay on his side with his face away from me. The rock his head lay against was stained red. My heart tripped in my chest, and my hand fluttered to cover my mouth.

I kneeled next to the massive bear and touched the soft fur on his arm. Warmth still radiated. I leaned my ear against his back, and after moving a few times, I picked up his heartbeat.

I let out the breath I had been holding and glanced at my father. "He's alive." I climbed to my feet and circled around to his other side. Gently, I lifted his head, inspecting the ugly gash on his brow that still oozed blood. The ground underneath his abdomen was sticky with it, and when I lifted his paw to see the damage, I winced at the jagged slices running across his stomach. They were deep enough to provide days of discomfort, but at least he had not been disemboweled.

"He needs help," I said, looking up at my father. My gaze turned to the pink and orange brushstrokes in the sky. When the sun set, Aiden would transform. I did not know the extent of the damage or if it would transform with him.

My father said nothing, but the corner of his lower lip sucked between his teeth.

A burn started in my blood at his quiet study of the situation, as if he were contemplating making me leave Aiden.

"He saved my life." My harsh whisper brought my father's gaze to mine. "He deserves amnesty."

"How do you expect us to get a five hundredweight, unconscious bear back to the castle?

I glanced at the darkening sky again. "In a few minutes, he will be a man, and I'm sure between the two of us, we can drag him back to the castle before daybreak."

His jaw tensed, and he glanced at the dead grizzly bear. "Fine," he conceded in a tone that was anything but peachy. "But he is going to the dungeon. I don't want an angry bear terrorizing the castle tomorrow."

"The dungeon is no place for an injured man. He can stay in my room where it is clean, and I can dress his wounds."

"And when the sun rises?" he snapped and crossed his arms.

"I'll give him honey and berries and make sure he doesn't break out to terrorize the castle."

The last rays of the sun faded from the sky, and Aiden's transformation took the form of a low glow. It wasn't the spectacle of the other night. This time, he shrank in place without the magnificent stretch or flexing of muscles.

He was just as unconscious as he was a moment ago.

My father's eyebrows rose and he balked. "Ye didn't tell me he'd be naked."

"Does it matter right now?" I asked, exasperated. I didn't want to argue with my father. All I wanted to do was get Aiden back to the castle and clean out his wounds. The longer we stayed here, the more likely he would come down with an infection. "Help me get him to his feet."

I slung his arm around my shoulder and pulled him into an awkward sitting position. The dead weight was almost too much to hold, and I nearly toppled over.

"Jesus, Mary, and Joseph, what are you doing, child?" my father muttered and reached down, yanking Aiden's other arm over his shoulder.

Together, we stood, both of us clasping our free arms around Aiden's blood-streaked waist. We skirted around the dead bear and started the long trek back to the castle, with Shadow at our heels.

# BRAVE Chapter 5

"WHAT IS THAT MAN doing in May's bed?" My mother didn't even try to keep her voice down in the hallway. "You know how dangerous having him near her is."

"You don't have to keep reminding me of my family's curse, woman." My father's low growl came through the door. "I am well aware of what a MacMahon could do to Marigold's descendant."

I washed the last of Aiden's wounds, and carefully covered it with a clean cloth as best I could. The pile of rags at my feet told more of the story than I cared to digest. I pulled the sheets over him, picked up the blood-and-grit filled cloths, and marched to the door with the evidence.

I flung it open and nearly threw the rags at my mother. "Father had no choice. Aiden saved my life, and I would not leave him to die out there. If Father hadn't helped me carry him, I would have dragged him here myself."

"What exactly do you think will happen when the sun comes up?"

I narrowed my eyes at my mother. "He is going to turn back into a bear."

"How will you contain him from terrorizing the castle?" My mother's voice rose to a near hysterical pitch.

"Honey and berries," I replied. We had had a long walk home supporting Aiden's weight, and I took that time to figure out what I would do in the morning. An injured animal of any kind was unpredictable, and while there was danger in having him in a confined space, I was confident I had this under control. "I already sent Sheri to get as much of both as she can find before the sun rises."

"We can have the guards bring him to the dungeon," my mother said.

"No. I'm not having them put him in that filth. Not when my bed is available and clean."

She opened her mouth.

"No." I turned and retreated into the room, closing the door on any further conversation.

Aiden looked peaceful as he slept. The gentle cadence of his breathing brought a sigh to my lips. I glanced down at my bloody hands and crossed to the basin.

After my hands were scrubbed clean, I changed out of the dirty night dress into something clean and warmer than the night shirt. I moved my vanity chair to the spot next to the bed and reached for Aiden's hand. My fingers traced his fingers, and the contact lit a fire deep within me. I turned his hand over and followed the intricate lines in his palm with my index finger. Each path led to his wrist, and there was an intimacy to my actions that left my breath shallow and my heart pumping.

The door opened, and I dropped his hand, pushing back in the chair while heat filled my cheeks.

Sheri stood in the doorway with a full tray of fruits and berries, along with a large stack of honeycombs.

"Thank you." I smiled and pointed to my dressing table. "You can put it there and then take your leave."

"You don't want me to stay, my lady?" Sheri asked as she put the tray down.

"No. While he isn't any danger now, I'm afraid that will not be the case in the morning." I met her wide-eyed stare. "But you can take Shadow with you for a while. I don't think it is prudent to have a wolf and a bear sharing the room, either." I smiled.

She curtseyed and gathered Shadow up in her arms before she left the room.

I turned back to Aiden and stared at his palm, just waiting for me to continue my exploration of the patterns. Tentatively, I started tracing the lines again, memorizing each curve and intersection.

The overriding sense of someone watching me settled in, and I glanced up at his face. His eyes were open, revealing that blue that captured my heart. His lips formed the slightest curve of a smile. Heat filled my face and soon flushed through my entire body. When I went to pull away, his hand grasped mine.

He winced at the movement and his eyes squeezed closed. "Jesus," he whispered, and his free hand reached towards the bandages on his head.

I grabbed his arm before he could disrupt them. "Don't."

He stopped and pried one eye open. "What happened?"

"You didn't win the fight with that bear, but at least he didn't kill you."

Aiden pulled his arm from my grip and tried to sit up.

"Please, just lay back before you start bleeding again." I stood and gently pressed his shoulders back down on my bed.

"Where am I?"

"In my bedroom," I said.

His eyes widened.

"My father and I dragged you back here. And I patched you up the best I could." I adjusted the sheet and met his questioning gaze. "It's okay. They aren't going to lock you up in the dungeon."

He glanced towards the window and the lightening sky. "I can't stay here." He attempted to rise again, wincing as he moved.

"Aye. You can." This time, I pushed him down with more force. "You are in no condition to be wandering the forest today. Besides, I have honey and berries. I think I can handle the bear."

He let out a high-pitched laugh. "You are insane."

"You were the one who saved me. You aren't going to hurt me."

Aiden pressed his lips together and stared at the canopy of my bed. "Why would you even chance it?" His gaze traveled to mine, the question in his eyes just as clear as his underlying pain.

Fueled by the memory of his searing kiss, I leaned in and pressed my lips to his. His soft groan sent liquid fire to the spot between my legs as our mouths opened, allowing the slow exploration of our tongues. I clamped my thighs together against the sudden wetness.

His hand threaded in my hair, holding me in place as the kiss transformed into something irresistible.

When his other hand skimmed over the flesh of my thigh, I pulled away with a gasp. He had navigated the fabric of my dress while we were kissing, and now his fingers found that sweet spot between my legs that erased logical thought from my head.

I stood in place as he rubbed my folds in slow circles. His blue eyes locked with mine as he plucked my body like a master minstrel. I let him bring me to the brink, and I pressed the back of my wrist to my mouth to stop the moan that wanted to escape as every muscle tightened and a warm rush coated his hand.

His fingers slid inside me, adding to my heat. My hips ground into his hand, demanding more. Aiden's eyes closed. His mouth parted, and a soft sigh slipped out. The sheet tented with the stiffness of his manhood and all I could imagine was that thick length filling me instead of his hand.

When his eyes opened, a raw need filled them, but he turned away, glancing at the window again. He pulled his hand from between my legs, and I let out a squeak of protest.

He drew his fingers into his mouth, sucking my juices from his flesh as he groaned. "You need to leave unless you want to be taken by a bear."

I stepped back. The warmth filling me turned frigid, and I blinked as his words sank through the lingering euphoria he had created.

"Go," he whispered. His voice filled with as much urgency as his eyes. When the nails on his finger grew into sharp claws, he rolled out of the bed, landing on the floor on the far side with a grunt.

I took a step towards the bed and a roar filled the room. Nails scraped wood. The arch of a brown-furred back appeared over the side of the mattress. The metallic taste of fear filled my mouth, but my feet still refused to leave the spot where I stood.

When the grizzly grew to his full height, the last of the bandages I had used fell to the ground. His sharp, blue-eyed gaze locked on me, reflecting that same intense want.

My feet finally listened to my brain, and I turned, running to the door.

Before I could get the knob turned, his enormous paw slammed on the wood, blocking my escape. His warm body pressed against mine, and his snout tickled my neck. His low, suggestive growl was beyond what I could take. I jabbed my elbow into his hurt side.

His teeth pressed down on the back of my neck.

The pressure froze me in place. "No. Aiden," I said. My voice was steady despite the tremors filling me from my toes all the way to where his sharp teeth dug into my soft flesh. "Let go."

To my surprise, the bear followed my demand and let me go. He backed up a few paces, and I turned to face him. He shook his head like he was shaking water off and roared at me.

I pointed my finger at him. "You are going to behave. Understand?"

He growled low, remaining on all fours, and huffed before he turned and assessed his surroundings. He circled and then settled on the floor to stare at me.

The howl outside my door made me jump, and as soon as my heart started up again, I rolled my eyes. I had to let my wolf in before he woke the entire castle. Without taking my eyes off Aiden, I cracked the door, and Shadow darted inside. I shut the door once he'd cleared.

Shadow slowed his gait, stopping a few steps in front of me. The hair on his neck rose, as did a vicious snarl from the back of his throat. He bared his teeth at the bear.

"It's okay, boy," I said and squatted, pulling the wolf to my side.

He calmed immediately and glanced back at me as if to make sure I was okay with the gigantic beast in the room. I stroked his back to make my point, and he turned to me, swathing my face with his tongue.

I sighed, pushing my wolf's snout away from my face. Now that I'd assured him there was no danger, Shadow turned and bounded in Aiden's direction with his tail up like he had found a new playmate.

Aiden climbed into a sitting position to where Shadow couldn't nip at his face. His gaze moved from the little thing weaving between his legs to mine, and he cocked his head as if to say, "Really?"

I smiled just as Shadow jumped onto Aiden's haunches. Aiden swatted Shadow, sending him rolling across the floor. But that only fueled the playfulness in my wolf pup. He ran straight at Aiden.

"He's just a puppy," I said before Aiden could snarl.

He glared at me and lay back down, resigned to the fact my dog was going to terrorize him all day. And it was going to be an endless day, at that.

# BRAVE Chapter 6

NOT ONLY WAS I ready to drop from exhaustion as the daylight faded away, I was ready to eat a holiday feast. I had shared the fruit with Aiden earlier, hand feeding the bear as Shadow bounced around, curious as to what we were doing. But as my grumbling abdomen made clear, that was not enough to sustain me. My stomach growled, even as my eyelids dipped. My head bobbed, and I jerked awake.

Shadow lay curled at my feet, and Aiden paced slowly in the cramped space. My bedroom was larger than most in the castle, but it was not big enough to allow for the restless roaming of the bear.

The click of nails was hypnotic, and I struggled to keep my eyes open.

Pressure on my shoulder yanked me awake. I shot up, straight in the chair I had been slumped in, and turned, gasping at the chiseled chest in front of me. I blinked and looked up into Aiden's amused smile.

"I have no idea how you could sleep through that ruckus," he said.

The churning noise in my belly was loud enough to rival Shadow's growls. But my wolf pup had, in fact, slept through the god-awful noise as well. I shrugged, and my gaze dropped to the silken throw blanket Aiden had tied around his waist.

"Any chance you could find me some clothes?" he asked.

"Aye." I yawned and stretched. When I went to stand, my head spun, and I stumbled.

Aiden caught me and sucked air through his teeth. He made sure I was steady, and then his hand went to the raw cuts on his side. At least they weren't oozing. There was something to be said about the healing abilities of transforming into a bear and back.

A soft knock on the door interrupted the moment. I stepped back out of his arms.

"Come in," I said as soon as I was sure my feet would hold me.

Sheri stepped inside with a tray overloaded with food and a bowl of milk for Shadow. My wolf pup stretched and trotted over to Sheri as if he thought all that food was for him. I didn't think I had ever been as grateful as I was at that moment.

"Thank you!" I followed her to the dressing table where she changed out the brimming tray with the empty one. "Think you can find something suitable for Aiden to wear?"

Her cheeks turned red as her gaze flitted to the nearly naked man in my room. "Are you sure?" she whispered in my ear.

I smiled and looked down at the floor before glancing at her sideways. She caught my dimples and suppressed a smile of her own.

"Aye, I'm sure," I whispered after a moment.

"Very well," she said and turned towards the door. Her gaze lingered on Aiden until she was out of sight.

Aiden put his hands on his hips and cocked an eyebrow at me. "You hesitated for a minute too long, my lady." He crossed and glanced at the array of meats and breads on the tray. "After you," he said, waving at the food.

Just his proximity clouded my thoughts. I picked at the food, unable to think of anything else but his hand between my legs last night.

His hands landed on my waist and I jumped.

"Are you just going to pick at that?" he whispered before running his tongue along the edge of my ear. "Because I have something much more interesting for you to eat than a tray full of food." His hands squeezed my hips, and he pressed against my back.

My heart fluttered, and my mouth went dry. I reached for the cup of wine, dousing the dryness in my mouth with the sweet concoction. I didn't dare turn, because the moment I faced the man, whatever logic remained in my mind would flee in favor of his lips.

"I'm undecided as to what to have first," I said and licked my lips, forcing myself to focus on the food instead of the steady pressure of his hands and the pleasant circle of his hips against mine. "Besides, Sheri will be back soon."

He purred in my ear, letting his tongue follow the line of my neck. It tickled and tantalized, and then it was gone, along with his touch. I glanced over my shoulder to catch him crossing to the window.

Aiden MacMahon had to be the sexiest man I had ever laid eyes on. The physical attraction was undeniable. But beyond his desire to bed me and to be free of the curse, I knew nothing about him. I took one of the chicken legs and turned in his direction.

"Tell me about yourself," I said.

Aiden turned, both his eyebrows arched. "Why?"

"Because I'd like to know more about you."

He laughed and looked out the window. "I'm not one of your suitor's, so there is no point in this conversation. Besides, it looks as though they are setting up for a beheading. Any bets on whose head will be on that chopping block?" He pointed to the courtyard.

I dropped the chicken leg on the plate and crossed to stand at his side. My eyes narrowed and my hands clenched. "That is not going to happen."

Shadow rubbed against my leg in a show of solidarity.

The door opened, and my father waltzed in with a couple of guards. Sheri was behind him with an armful of clothing, her face as shocked as mine felt.

"I see our prisoner has woken."

"He is not a prisoner." I stepped in front of Aiden, blocking him behind me. "He saved my life. Both our lives."

"We are not doing this, May," my father said through clenched teeth. "Take him to the gallows."

The guards started towards Aiden.

"No." I stood tall. "You told me to choose a husband. I choose Aiden. If you kill him, I will follow him into the afterlife, and I will take you with me."

No one in the room moved. My father stared at me with his jaw hanging open. Sheri clutched the clothing to her chest with her eyes as wide as I had ever seen them, and the guards stared at me in the same shocked expression everyone else wore.

"Leave my bedroom. Now." The resoluteness in my command was unmistakable.

The guards took a step back, unsure of what to do next. I glared at my father. The gauntlet had been issued, but my heart thundered in my chest at the indecision I saw in his eyes.

He glanced at Aiden and sneered.

My chest tightened, but I kept my face neutral, praying my fear didn't seep through my façade.

My father nodded at the guards.

They stepped forward, grabbing my arm, and pulled me along with Aiden out of the room. The king held up his hand before we passed and stared into my eyes.

"When you issue a threat, you better damn well be willing to follow through with it," he said to me and then pointed at the door.

I didn't speak. I didn't argue, even as they marched both of us to the courtyard where a small crowd had gathered for the beheading festivities. Anger festered inside me, creating a potent cocktail that swirled in my blood.

Aiden hadn't said a word since we were dragged from the room. I glanced at him as we were lined up side by side. My blanket still hung from him, but it had slipped enough for me to make out the sharp outline of his hips.

He glanced at me as they put another wooden block in the space in front of me.

A hush fell on the crowd.

I ripped my arm from the guard's grip and took a step forward, dropping to my knees in front of the chopping block. "If this is a world that persecutes a man just because he carries a name that was outlawed over a hundred years ago, I do not wish to be a part of it." My voice projected over the crowd. I lay my cheek on the wood and looked up at Aiden.

He slowly dropped to his knee and adopted the same position, his eyes locked with mine.

I reached my hand out, and he threaded his fingers through mine.

A disturbance started in the back of the courtyard. The crowd that had been so ripe for a killing turned.

"Why is Princess May up there?" someone in the crowd called out.

Their rumblings grew louder until my father climbed up on the stage.

"She chose a MacMahon." He pointed at Aiden.

"So what?" several of the people in the gathering called out.

"That's a ridiculous law," others chimed in.

"It doesn't warrant death!" still more yelled.

"I would have chosen him, too." A few catcalls echoed from the back.

Aiden blushed, but kept his gaze on me, our hands still intertwined as the masses argued our fates.

"You are the king. You can change the laws of the land."

I broke eye contact with Aiden and looked up, straight into Sheri's upturned face as she repeated verbatim the words I had said the morning after the feast. She still clung to the pile of clothing I had asked her to retrieve.

"You cannot kill your only daughter and strip this land of a future queen full of the kind of grace this nation needs. One with a heart so pure that only she would think of saving a wolf pup from certain destruction. You cannot deprive this land of a ruler who will deliver swift justice as effortlessly as a worthy pardon. Not for a century old grudge that no longer has meaning!" Her impassioned plea riled the crowd further.

She had been there for me time and time again over the years and was my closest and strongest advocate outside of my parents. It humbled me that she would stick her neck out for me in such a public way.

My father stood clenching and unclenching his fists as he scanned the crowd. He crossed to the axe and picked it up, then positioned himself before lining up the blade with Aiden's neck.

I leaned back on my heels, still holding Aiden's hand. He didn't move from his position, nor did his eyes leave me. He squeezed my hand tighter, waiting for the end.

My father raised the blade in the air.

"Do not do this," I said, my voice low with a warning thrum I had never heard.

My father hesitated and moved his focus to me.

His eyes widened the same way the guard who unlocked the dungeon cell for me had.

The crowd gasped and fell silent.

I didn't dare move my gaze from my father's, but Aiden's hand squeezed in a way that defined involuntary shock.

My father slowly lowered the axe and took a shaky step back. The color bled from his face, leaving him pasty under the shadow of the moon.

I glanced at Aiden. He wasn't looking at me, but beyond me with eyes wide with fear. His grip on my hand tightened.

Metal hit wood. My gaze snapped back to my father. The blade of the axe stuck out of the wood deck at his feet. The echo of the bang was enough to snap everyone out of what had bewitched them.

"Bring them to the throne room," my father said, low enough for only the guards to hear, and then he stormed out of the courtyard.

# BRAVE Chapter 7

AIDEN AND I WERE dragged into the empty throne room and forced to our knees. A blade was held at each of our throats, keeping us in place.

My father stepped into the room, his normal, calm demeanor gone. His face was as red as I had ever seen it, and his hands were in fists so tight they were almost white. He paced the floor with his lips pressed into a thin line. His eyes bore through me.

Nearly two minutes of silence went by before he spoke. "Put the swords away," he growled.

The blade under my chin disappeared, and I slouched as the stress keeping me upright evaporated. Aiden reached for me.

"Do not touch her," my father snarled, then he turned his brutal glare my way. "What the hell did you do out there?

I blinked at him. "I told you not to kill Aiden."

"You conjured a ghost!" His bellow echoed in the great hall.

"I most certainly did not."

"There was a spirit surrounding you," Aiden said.

"Why would you call that...that thing?"

I stared at my father. "I did not call any spirit." My heart hammered in my chest as I glanced between my father and Aiden. "On my mother's life," I added, raising my hand to make my oath have more impact.

"Do you swear on his life?" My father pointed at Aiden.

"Aye." I didn't dare lose eye contact with him, because the moment I looked away, he would mistake it for a lie.

He stopped pacing and deflated before my eyes. His gaze shifted to Aiden. "If she didn't conjure that ghost, you must have."

Aiden laughed, and the guard closest to him jabbed the blunt end of his sword into Aiden's side. His laugh caught in his throat as he doubled over in pain. His head touched the ground while he wrapped his arms around his midsection.

"Did you curse her?" Father pointed at me, his voice bouncing off the stately rock pillars.

"No." Aiden gasped and pulled himself back onto his knees with narrowed eyes. "Did you?"

My father blinked and slowly took a seat on his throne. Defeat creased his brow, and he ran his hand down his face. The way his gaze traveled between the two of us bloomed hope in my heart.

He glanced at the guards. "Leave us."

The guards left us alone in the room.

"Get dressed," my father ordered Aiden, pointing to the pile of clothing Sheri had left behind.

Aiden climbed to his feet and crossed to the clothing. I tried not to let my gaze wander in his direction, but I couldn't help it. My insides clenched with disappointment as a shirt covered his bare back, and I looked away.

My father was studying me from his perch, and when Aiden crossed and offered me his hand, I took it, despite the tightening of my father's jaw. Aiden helped me to my feet, and then we both turned to my father.

With our hands still clasped, Aiden cocked his head. "Did you curse her?"

"Perhaps I did, but not by intention," he said softly. "Just as your family has been cursed all these years, Marigold's wrath may have wrapped itself around the only female descendant to grace the Stewart line since her death." His sharp stare landed on me. "There is more to the story than just the cursing of the MacMahons."

Aiden squeezed my hand and glanced at me out of the corner of his eyes. Heat rose in my cheeks, and I licked my lips before pressing them together. I shifted my weight and focused on my father.

He leaned forward and rested his elbows on his knees, studying the floor. With a sigh, he looked up. "I did not want to believe the lore." His gaze passed over the two of us and traveled up the columns to the ornate colors painted on the ceiling. "But I should have known better when I saw you at the castle." His eyes locked on Aiden, and he shook his head slowly.

I shifted closer to Aiden, my body trembling under the tension. Nerves bit at my skin, and the longer my father remained quiet, the more demanding the sensation became. Aiden's grip on my hand tightened, calming me.

The fog that clouded my father's eyes cleared, and he stood, his face changing back to that hard resolve that made my stomach sink.

"I will make a deal with you," he said, staring at Aiden. "I will recant the law that makes your name a capital offense, and in return, you will leave this castle and never return."

My stomach dropped.

Aiden's hand squeezed tight, and he glanced at me. The longing in his eyes produced a physical pain in my chest, as if my heart had been ripped from my body. When his grip loosened, letting my hand go, I thought my legs would fail.

"And if I refuse?" Aiden said.

"Then you die today, regardless of what my daughter says."

I balked at my father, my jaw hanging open as my brain stalled. Did he not see what had just happened in the courtyard?

Aiden stared at the ground. The corner of his lip sucked between his teeth as he glanced at me. The fact he was contemplating his choices tightened my throat.

"Accept the deal and go," I whispered. I couldn't imagine living in a world where he wasn't alive.

He nodded. "Fine. I accept your terms." His voice cracked, and his hands curled into fists as if his body did not agree to his promise. "Can I say a proper goodbye?"

My father waved for him to proceed.

Aiden turned to me, his blue eyes reflecting the sadness in his down-turned lips. He closed the distance and wrapped his arms around me, hugging me tight. His lips pressed against the top of my head. "Goodbye, May," he whispered and then stepped away, turning and heading out of the throne room.

When the door opened, the guards blocked his exit.

"Let him go. I am recanting the law that calls for his death," my father announced.

The guards let Aiden pass.

I watched until he disappeared around the corner, waiting for him to glance back, but he never did. I spun, sending a glare at my father. "Why?" was all I could muster.

The doors of the great hall closed, and my father looked down at me. "Because a union between a MacMahon and a Stewart is forbidden." He stood and came down the steps to stand in front of me. He placed his hands gently on my shoulders. "It cannot be."

"Why?" I yelled and knocked his hands away from me. The anger built inside me, making my skin tingle.

"Because it will bring Marigold back from the dead, and she vowed to destroy everything the Stewarts loved." His lips pressed together as he gripped my arms. "Do you love that monster?"

I recoiled, but my father didn't let go. "He isn't a monster." My voice was breathless as the anger transformed into fear.

"Do you love him?"

My gaze darted around the room. I had only known him for a few days, but the squeezing of my heart told me the truth. While I knew little about Aiden MacMahon, I had been ready to join him in the afterlife.

"Why would Marigold destroy everything we love?" I didn't understand where this conversation was going, and I wasn't ready to admit I loved the man. At least, not to my father.

"Because as soon as Marigold gave birth to an heir, my great, great, great grandfather had her burned at the stake for witchcraft. Her dying decree was that she would destroy the house of Stewart as surely as they had destroyed the house of MacMahon. The firstborn female in the house of Stewart would be hers to command, and the two houses would collide, bringing forth ultimate destruction."

It sounded a little too cryptic to me. At least with Aiden's curse, the cure was much clearer than the witch's dying rant.

"You are the first female born to a Stewart since Marigold burned at the stake. And the fact that her ghost appeared out there..." He nodded his chin towards the courtyard and shook his head. "I cannot take the chance of that witch destroying you or your mother."

The mention of my mother made me stiffen.

"All that I love," my father whispered.

I thought of all I truly loved, and my heart squeezed. Aiden was included, alongside my parents and Sheri.

"How do we stop this?" I whispered, afraid that the door allowing Marigold in may have already been opened.

"You are to never see that man again."

# BRAVE Chapter 8

I LAY IN BED thinking about all my father had said. The idea of never seeing Aiden, of never feeling his lips on mine or his hands on my body, left me cold.

Doubt laced itself into everything my father had told me. I rolled to my side, staring out the window at the dawn's soft light. My longing for Aiden was greater than my fear that my father's story was real.

After a near sleepless night, I climbed out of bed and made my way to the dining hall for breakfast. The only activity in the room was the servants bringing the food in. I piled my plate with sweet breads and meats before sitting down to graze.

My parents came in just as I had swallowed my last bite.

"I'm going back to bed." I stood as they sat. "I didn't get any sleep last night."

"Are you feeling all right?" my mother asked.

I nodded. "Just exhausted." I headed to my room.

While I was tired, I needed to buy myself some time. With Shadow on my heels, I dressed in my warmest hunting outfit, donning pants instead of a skirt, and put pillows under the covers so if anyone looked into the room, it would look like someone was in the bed.

I tucked my hair up under a woolen hat and slid Shadow into a bag before I took my bow and arrow from the back corner. When I slid out of the room, I kept my head down so no one would recognize me.

A group of men were heading out, and I trailed them. Not one guard paid me any attention. They assumed I was with the group of hunters. As soon as we hit the woods, the men went straight, and I peeled off to the right, keeping my steps as quiet as I could. I tried to remember my hunting track from the other day. I needed to find that field, as well as that barricade that had stopped me.

When I could no longer hear the men I had exited the castle with, I let Shadow out of my bag. He walked alongside me, sometimes bounding ahead, only to stop and look back. I crouched and slipped him a piece of meat I had taken from the hall. He ate it in one bite.

"Find Aiden," I whispered, and his ears perked up. "Find the bear."

His tail wagged, and he turned, putting his nose to the ground like he had understood my request. I followed his zigzag pattern, letting him lead me through the thickening woods.

We came upon the small glen where I had first seen Aiden. Shadow skirted the nest of bushes, finding a small space to make his way through. I dropped to my knees and looked through the opening. Shadow looked back at me from the other side. I sighed and pushed my bow and quiver through and then got down on my stomach.

I wiggled my way through the opening like an inchworm. It took what seemed like forever, but when I got to the opening, Shadow licked my face and moved back, allowing me to crawl to my hands and knees. I kneeled in the small space. The entire alcove was blocked by gnarled bushes. In the far corner, a dark opening caught my attention.

Shadow was already heading that way. My heart pumped raw adrenaline through my veins as I crawled towards the opening of the cave. Shadow stood at the entrance with his nose in the air. He bounded into the darkness. I scrambled after him.

The blackness of the cave was broken only by Aiden's wide blue eyes, that seemed to glow. Shadow's panting and scraping of nails against rock were the only sounds in the space. I blinked, forcing my eyes to adjust to the dark.

A low rumbling in the bear's chest caught me off guard, and then I remembered the hat. I pulled it off, and my hair fell in loose curls. The growl stopped, and a huff filled the space. His blue eyes kept me entranced as they moved closer.

"Hunters in the woods," I whispered.

His gaze jerked towards the entrance.

"They didn't follow me. No one knows I'm here."

Aiden turned and lumbered deeper into the cavern. I hesitated, but Shadow followed as if being near a large grizzly bear was normal. With my vision slowly adjusting, I carefully made my way in the direction I thought they had gone, shuffling my feet so I could navigate around any rocks I came in contact with instead of tripping over something.

Shadow came back to my side and nudged my knee before bounding back into the darkness. As I walked, my eyes seemed to adjust. Either that or the cave was getting lighter. Rushing water filled my ears. I skirted around a boulder, stepping into a larger cave with a small waterfall. It was warm here, like a mid-summer day, and the water glowed, filling the space with blue light.

Aiden stood knee-deep in the water and batted a fish onto the rocky shore near where I stood. The second it hit the ground, Shadow was on it, tearing flesh from bone and eating his fill. Several fish skeletons lay in the far corner with a fire pit that lay barren of wood or ash. A small straw bed sat near the fire, along with clothing drying on the rocks.

This was Aiden's home. I studied the walls and the crystals hanging on the ceiling that seemed to carry their own warm glow. I couldn't imagine the bear fitting into the underbrush clearing that I had crawled through to get inside the cavern, nor could I imagine Aiden doing the same.

"Is that the only way in here?" I pointed to the cavern where we had come in.

Aiden was too focused on the task at hand and dove for another fish. He came up with it in his mouth. It disappeared between his teeth, and he lumbered onto shore, shaking off the water. Warm spray doused me. He crossed to the corner opposite the bed and made himself comfortable.

My gaze turned to the straw mat, and I yawned. "I didn't sleep last night at all. Mind if I lie down?" I pointed to the bedding.

Aiden huffed.

I took that as a yes and crossed to the bed, took off my shoes, and curled up on the soft straw. His scent filled the space, and before I knew it, my eyes closed.

CRACKLING WARMTH PULLED ME from sleep. Aiden, in his human form, kneeled next to a roaring fire with a spit filled with fish cooking over it. His bare back faced me, and I reached out, running my fingers over his skin.

He jerked and looked over his shoulder. "Good morning." He smiled.

"Don't you mean good evening?" I stretched my aching muscles.

Shadow stretched, too, from his perch next to me and then licked my face.

I sat up, pushing my wolf pup away. The cave still glowed with an ethereal light. It reminded me of Aiden's eyes.

"So, this is where you live?" I twirled my finger around.

He pulled a crude plate from a shelf in the wall and dropped the cooked fish on it. He handed me the plate and sat back, leaning against the rock next to the bedding and stretching his leather-clad legs towards the fire.

"Why did you come?" he asked after I started picking at the dinner he had served me.

"I can leave if you want me to." I put the plate down on the bed between us and stood.

"If I wanted you to leave, I wouldn't have cooked you breakfast." He raised an eyebrow at me.

I sat back down and returned my focus on the food. Cooked salmon always tasted delicious, and these were beyond fresh. The fish melted in my mouth and I shared a few morsels with Shadow. When the bones were picked clean, I handed Aiden the plate.

Despite the fish carcasses lying about, the cave didn't stink with the stench of decaying flesh. Instead, it smelled like honey and spring rain. I climbed to my feet, crossed to the water, and crouched down to wash my hands. It was hot, like a newly drawn bath. I glanced over my shoulder.

"It's a hot spring, but the center is deep and cold. That's the channel where the fish swim through."

I cocked an eyebrow and stood, shaking the warm water from my hands before wiping them on my hips. Aiden climbed to his feet and crossed to me.

"Why did you come?" he asked, his voice soft and tender. His fingers brushed my cheek, tucking the stray hairs behind my ear.

"You know why," I said, breathless from his touch. Every cell in my body wanted him. I couldn't deny this strong connection.

He leaned in, and his lips crushed against mine. His arms wrapped around my waist, pulling me against his hard chest. The kiss transcended, making my body vibrate with need. I wanted to feel that same freedom, that same high I felt in my bedroom. I wanted all of Aiden.

He broke the kiss and stared down at me. "I can never set foot in the castle."

"I don't care." My hands trailed down his chest to the clasp of his pants.

He grabbed my wrists, holding them still. The carnal need in his eyes and the tension in his face belied his motion. "I am a bear by day," he said, his voice quivering.

"I don't care."

"My offspring are cursed as well," he said and stepped back. "I do not wish this life on anyone."

I stared at him, measuring the need pumping through my blood and the desire so clearly outlined in the fabric of his pants. My fingers nimbly unbuttoned the shirt I wore. I stripped the fabric from my shoulders and tossed it aside.

Aiden groaned at the sight of my bare breasts. "Please, May," he whispered.

His eyes begged me. For what, I wasn't sure. I peeled off my pants and stood at the edge of the water without a stitch of clothing on.

His pupils dilated, leaving only a thin edge of blue around the black abyss. His fingers fumbled with the clasp on his pants. He closed his eyes and pulled his hands away, clenching them.

I closed the distance, placing my palms on his chest. His heart raced underneath my hands, and his eyes jerked open. His breathing quickened. He stared down at me, trembling under my touch.

"Don't you want me?" I asked in a hushed whisper, laying my vulnerability at his feet.

With a guttural growl, he tore his pants off and then had me in his arms as he walked us into the water. His lips captured mine, walking us backwards until I lost my footing. He continued until the heat vanished and all that wrapped around us was the frigid depths of the water. He pulled away from my lips, his breathing ragged. When I wrapped my legs around his waist, his eyes clamped closed and his lips pressed together.

He pushed beyond the cold, into warmer waters on the inside of the cave lake, near the waterfall. He lifted me onto a rock and kissed me deeper than he had ever done before. I shook with need. When the kiss broke, I whined, but his lips trailed down my cheek to my throat. The sensation of his tongue swiping my skin and his butterfly kisses pulled a moan from deep inside me.

His mouth attacked each breast as if they were his only sustenance, nipping, licking, sucking until I thought I would go insane. Every sensation brought forth a cry from my lips.

With a wicked grin, he moved lower, kissing my belly, and running his tongue in a circle in my belly button. He pushed my legs wider, and I thought my heart would explode when his mouth clamped down on the spot his fingers had manipulated the other night.

His tongue was more magical, more commanding, than his hands had been. I laced my fingers through his hair, keeping him in the spot that produced the most decadent sounds from my mouth. So much so, that Shadow howled from the other side of the lake.

Aiden chuckled, his hot breath making me shiver. He glanced up at me and grinned as he gently nibbled. He pushed his fingers inside my hot path and wiggled them, creating delicious waves through my entire form.

Muscles tightened, and a heat so strong wrapped itself around me. I cried out his name, relishing the way it echoed on the rocks surrounding us as a rush of wetness flowed from between my legs.

Aiden's hands and mouth left my skin, and he stood with my fingers still entangled in his hair. The tip of his hard member brushed my sensitive nub, and then he plunged his hips forward, sending his hardness deep inside me.

I gasped as pain and pleasure collided. My eyes widened, as did his smile. He gripped my hips, pushing himself farther inside me until our bodies touched. Aiden's eyes closed, his head fell back, and his mouth parted in a pleasured sigh.

I yanked his head towards me, crushing his lips to mine, and he twisted, pulling me off the rock and into the warm water. My back slammed against the side of the rock with the force of his thrust. I arched into him, crying out into his mouth. Our frantic rhythm created waves in the pool, and grunts of exertion sounded from both of us.

Our lovemaking was on the verge of violent, but it brought me beyond this realm, filling me with power like I had never experienced before. Intense sensations filled every pore of my body. A grinding twirl of my hips or raking my nails across his back brought forth pleasure as a growl with my name on it.

Intense heat flushed through me, tightening my muscles, and I tilted my head back with a scream of satisfaction as I peaked. His mouth clamped on my throat as he rode me hard through each wave of ecstasy until he plunged deeper than he had before and cried my name to the gods as his hot seed filled me.

Trembling, he held me tight, still coupled, his head resting on my shoulder and his chest heaved in time with mine. I kissed the spot where his neck and shoulder met, and his flesh transitioned into a map of gooseflesh.

He lifted his head and captured a gentle kiss, sucking my lower lip between his teeth.

He uncoupled from me, and the sudden emptiness sent an ache through my body. Taking my hand, he led me under the waterfall. The chill in the falling water invigorated me, and I stepped close to his warmth, letting the water soak through every strand of hair.

Aiden tilted his head back under the deluge before rubbing his face. He stepped behind the waterfall into another cozy alcove.

As soon as I stepped behind the wall of water, Shadow howled in discontent from the other shore. I poked my head back through. "Shush. We are right here."

The wolf pup climbed up on the bedding and curled up in a sulk only I could read. His eyes locked on our location.

I crossed into the alcove and ran my hands through my hair, smoothing it away from my face. It was darker in this space without the glow from the pool or the crystals at the top of the cavern.

Aiden leaned against a rock, his legs crossed as well as his arms. He stared at the ground.

I stepped closer, and his gaze flicked up, stopping me in place. It was hard and full of resolve.

My heart recoiled, and I wrapped my arms over my exposed chest.

"We can't..." He closed his eyes and ran his hands through his hair. "Damn it, May," he snarled. "We just can't." He waved towards the waterfall. His jaw tensed as he stared at me.

My chest hurt. I had given him everything in that moment, and he stood here rejecting me. My eyes stung, and I turned away before he could see the tears that I fought back.

"Aw, fuck," he whispered. A moment later, his hands landed on my shoulders. He gripped them tight and pressed a kiss on the top of my head. "My mother died giving birth to me. All the MacMahon women die in childbirth. I just can't..." His chin pressed down on my head, and his arms wrapped around me. "Just like I can't even consider the cure."

I turned in his arms, looking up at him. The hardness in his eyes had been replaced with melancholy.

He nodded towards the waterfall. "That can't happen again. I lost complete control, and it is too dangerous for you."

My insides twisted with disappointment. "And what if I want to take the risk?"

He smoothed my hair back and planted a gentle kiss. "No. You dying is not a risk I'm willing to take. Even though I had a taste of heaven that I'll crave for the rest of my life, I can't."

My heart wanted Aiden.

My body wanted Aiden.

My soul wanted Aiden.

Anger bloomed inside me at the injustice, and power flooded through my veins with it. The surrounding air swirled and before I could utter a sound, it pierced through my back like a lance, filling my form and shutting my voice down. I was trapped in my body.

Aiden stepped back, his eyes wide with horror. "May?"

The cackling laugh coming from my mouth made me shiver. *"Parere me."*

Marigold's ghostly voice flowed from me. The words formed a mystical fog that surrounded Aiden.

He stiffened when it pierced his skin, seeping into him like a fatal disease. His eyes muted gray. I struggled to get loose of Marigold's mental grip. Pain flashed in my head.

"Silly girl, you cannot break my hold. Righteous anger let me in, and now I control your flesh as well as your lover's." My form sauntered to Aiden.

He looked down at me with gray, lifeless eyes. I screamed.

# BRAVE Chapter 9

MARIGOLD WAS INSATIABLE. Demanding Aiden perform until he finally fell into an exhausted stupor just before sunrise. I was bruised and battered from his voraciousness, and while I was locked inside my mind, I still felt the pain accosting every muscle.

Shadow had fled the area, shaking and soiling himself from the cavern entry as he watched. He sensed the evil and whined every time Marigold spoke. I hoped Aiden could break free once he was in bear form, but the sinking feeling in my stomach told me that was wishful thinking.

The night transitioned to morning, and Aiden transformed. His bear still slept where he had fallen. Marigold strutted around him, her hands rubbing the beast's fur. The softness of it clung to my skin, squeezing my heart further.

"Oh, to be mounted by such a mighty beast," she whispered with such curiosity that I gasped. Her intentions terrified me.

Aiden stirred and swung his massive head in my direction. His eyes reflected that same muted gray. I shivered.

Marigold still wielded power over him, even while in bear form. She crossed to one boulder and draped herself over it. Inviting the bear without words.

He crossed to where Marigold had me draped, and he sniffed at me. He turned, heading towards the water.

Marigold snarled within me. "*Tolle eam.*"

The bear stiffened and turned in such a stilted manner, I thought he would break. As he started towards me, Shadow darted from his hiding place and put himself between the bear and where I lay. My wolf growled with such heinous intent that my heart leaped into my throat.

I couldn't tell him he was a good wolf. I couldn't tell him to get out of the way, either.

Aiden's paw swiped at the little thing.

Shadow buried his teeth in Aiden's paw. Aiden bellowed in pain, trying to shake off the wolf. His eyes flashed blue for a moment, and Shadow released, flying into the lake from the inertia. The wolf surfaced and swam to shore, then shook and slunk back into the dark.

Aiden licked his paw, showing no interest in me. When he glanced over, the blue was gone from his irises and only gray remained. Still, he didn't approach me. He didn't conform to Marigold's command.

"*Tolle eam*," she yelled, still holding my body against the rock, like a drunk harlot looking for action. She wiggled my butt.

That got his attention. Interest flashed across his bear features. He lumbered over and climbed on my back. The weight of him yanked the air from my lungs, nearly crushing me.

"*Prohibere!*" Marigold squeezed out, stopping Aiden before he started. As the bear retreated, Marigold stood and turned, regarding him with disgust. "We can't have your precious girl being crushed to death before the eclipse. That would ruin my fun."

*The eclipse?*

"Aye. Today is the day we die trying to break the MacMahon curse." She cackled, and a wave of gooseflesh covered my bare arms. "If you hadn't provided me with the perfect entrance, I would have had to take you by force as you slept."

Aiden's eyes flashed for a moment, and then that obedient gray overshadowed them.

Marigold picked up my discarded clothing, sneering at the pants and shirt. "What kind of clothing is this?"

*It's my hunting outfit.*

"Well, we will just have to make do." She glanced at Aiden's shirt hanging over the rock and dropped my clothing. The soft fabric caressed my skin with his honey scent as Marigold put the shirt on. It fell to just above my knees. She grabbed his belt and fastened it around my waist. "This will do far better than your hideous hunting outfit." She pulled on my boots to complete the outfit and glanced at Aiden. "It is time to head to Stonehenge. Lead the way, mighty beast."

He lumbered past where I stood, and Marigold followed, forcing my muscles to obey her nefarious order. I already knew what the ritual entailed. The thought of Aiden drinking enough of my blood to leave me on the brink between life and death turned my stomach.

"Child, he will drink every drop. He will not stop until your heart does," Marigold whispered.

My lips spread in a smile that was not my own, and I struggled to break free of Marigold's mental grip.

The path out of the cave was not as hard to navigate as the path I used coming in, although the entrance was hidden behind a large patch of prickly bushes.

We stepped into the thinning woods. The sunshine played between the leaves. Bright rays dotted our path until the woods gave way to an open field. The sight of my father's army surrounding the majestic stones was welcomed. He must have found me gone during the night and sent his men out to stand watch. A piece of me rejoiced. Marigold didn't have a prayer of making it through the crowded field.

Aiden stopped at the edge of the woods, and Marigold stepped beside him, putting her hand on his head. His soft fur tickled my palm.

"*Invisibilia*," Marigold whispered and then stepped into the open glen.

I kept waiting for someone to see us, but she navigated through the men like we really were invisible.

When we stepped into the great circle, she turned and put her hands up. *"Praesidio!"*

The space around the rocks shimmered with her protection spell, and my heart sank. Shadow ran from the wood line, weaving in and out of the guards as they moved. They nearly tripped on each other as the wolf pup navigated the same path we took. The moment my dog came in contact with the barrier, his little form was thrown back ten feet.

"No!" I cried, but it was only in my head. Marigold's laugh was the only thing flowing from my mouth.

Shadow climbed unsteadily to his feet and let out a heart-wrenching howl. The guard close to him drew his sword, intending to take down my furry friend. I cringed as the blade whistled towards Shadow, but it met the unyielding steel of my father's sword.

He glanced up at me through the shimmering barrier, his expression stoic.

"Let them go, Marigold!" he called, his gaze narrowing.

The witch keeping me captive laughed and turned away, dismissing my father in a way I would never dream of. She propelled my form forward, nearly throwing me onto a flat stone in the middle of the array.

She sat me up like an old rag doll, spreading my legs wide so my calves dangled over the edges of the rock. Leaning back on my palms, she said, "Come here, my beast." She raised my shirt high enough to give Aiden, along with anyone beyond the barrier, quite the view. "Time to hunt for some honey with that tongue of yours," she purred.

I cringed and renewed my mental struggle.

Aiden climbed onto the rock with his front legs and stuck his snout between my thighs, obeying the order. Mortification crept through me, but Marigold kept that hideous smile on my face and glared at my father. Her satisfaction as his face turned red zipped through me.

I growled and forced my body to respond. My hips bucked, and my hands slipped, knocking the witch backwards. Our head connected with the rock, sending a dizzying wave through me.

Aiden's head snapped up, his eyes wide, and blue flashed for a moment. He was struggling to gain control, just like I was.

Marigold screamed in frustration, shooting my right arm over the edge of the rock. The sky above us darkened as shadows began blocking the sun.

"*Indicem minibus apertum carpi ulnaris!*"

Aiden hopped off the rock and crossed to my wrist. His teeth flashed and captured my flesh between them, slicing to the bone.

I screamed, but the sound never left my head.

"*Absorptio!*" Marigold cried.

His mouth clamped down, drinking my blood with such fervor that my head spun. For a moment, the fact the sky was near black didn't register. The pain in my arm was too great. My heart slammed in my chest, each beat weaker with the bear suckling my blood.

The moment the moon blocked the sun in totality, Aiden transitioned to man. His grip on my arm was as feral as the bears had been. He consumed my blood in large pulls, sucking, swallowing.

His gaze moved to mine, and despite Marigold's hold on both of us, I saw the desperation in the gray-blue of his irises. Marigold just laughed as he drained my body.

The world swam. My father's cries from outside the protection spell echoed in the space around us. Shadow's mewing matched that of Aiden's.

When Marigold grabbed Aiden's hand and placed it between my legs, he actually cringed, but that didn't stop his fingers from their slow swirl on the spot that his tongue had played with last night before Marigold had taken over.

The gray in Aiden's eyes faded, replaced by a sheen of tears. Yet he kept pulling blood from my mangled arm, swallowing my life in greedy slurps. He silently pleaded for me to hold on, for me not to die before the moon passed through the sun.

I could see it in his soul. I could feel it in his fingers as they played gently with me, fueling my adrenaline, pumping my heart harder. Killing me faster.

When a tear slid down his cheek, I knew he had no control. This was the curse itself driving him. This was Marigold in her finest hour.

Marigold's laugh continued as my vision faded. Rays of the sun hit Aiden, and he closed his eyes. The strength of his drinking lessened. His teeth dislodged from my flesh, but his lips remained on my skin. His tongue swiped back and forth over my torn flesh as if his motion could bandage the damage.

Tears flowed from his blue eyes as he opened them and stared into mine. Pain etched his face as the sun bathed him in light. He forced his hand from between my legs, the strain of it tightening the muscles in his neck, and he cradled my arm in both of his, sobbing.

The slowing of my heart pounded in my ears.

"Aiden," I forced out between Marigold's cackles.

He pulled his mouth away from my arm, momentarily gaining control, just like I had. "Don't die."

Then Marigold took control again, forcing his mouth to cover the wound once more.

His request was a tall order, especially since darkness had already taken control over the edges of my vision.

Aiden jerked away. "NO!" he cried to the heavens, still cradling my limb. His grip on my upper arm tightened like a noose.

"*Et abiit suppeditat animus cupidine!*" The cry came from outside the protection spell.

With the last of my strength, I turned my head and looked straight into my mother's eyes. My father kneeled before her with a knife to his throat. Tears cascaded down my mother's face.

"*Accipere sacrificium meum,*" my father said.

The knife slid across my father's throat. I gasped. Blood splattered the ground in front of him. Marigold, being the greedy witch she was, favored the king's body over mine. She fled with such force that my body jerked from the rock, yanking a cry of pain from my lips.

Aiden collapsed on the ground, and Shadow darted through the space now that Marigold's protection spell had been broken. My arm ached, and the light around me faded. I heard nothing above the buzzing in my ears.

I stared at the reanimated body of my father and blinked, trying to make sense of what I was seeing. A blade flashed and severed the head from the body, but what rolled on the ground did not look like my father. It looked like the prize pig from our stable.

More words were uttered, and then a flame lowered from a familiar hand between the rocks, lighting the pig's head on fire. My father glanced at me, the torch in his hand, his expression stoic and hard.

A yank at my waist focused my attention behind me. I stared at Aiden as he ripped the belt from around me.

He looked beautiful in the sunlight, his eyes bluer than the sky above.

"Aiden," I whispered, and his gaze found mine.

The brightness at the edges of my vision grew. A jerk on my upper arm pinched. The light filtered over everything, and even Aiden's blue eyes faded into the white.

# BRAVE Chapter 10

"IF SHE NEEDS MORE, she can have more!" Aiden's voice penetrated the blackness surrounding me.

"If you continue, you will die."

I didn't recognize that voice, but the words hit hard. "Don't die." I forced the whisper from my lips.

Silence and then feet shuffling about the room. Pain registered in my arm.

"Hold this tight," that strange voice said.

My fingers tingled with the pressure being applied to my arm. I tried to open my eyes, but all I saw were glimpses through my thick lashes before my lids would become uncooperative again.

"Come on, May. I know you're in there," Aiden whispered, pulling me farther out of the black.

My eyelids fluttered again. Aiden's blue eyes came into focus. He looked haggard and pale.

"There's my princess," he said softly.

I glanced at my arm. His thumb pressed down on a bandage over the inside of my elbow. He had the same peculiar bandage on the inside of his arm that he was also applying pressure on. Rough stitches traversed my lower arm and wrist. No wonder my entire arm hurt so much.

Memories flashed before my eyes, and my gaze snapped up to Aiden. "The cure," I whispered, feeling felt like someone stuffed my mouth with wool.

He smiled crookedly, and some color bloomed in his cheeks. "That...well, aye, it seems to have worked."

"And Marigold?"

"Gone."

I lay back on the pillow and closed my eyes, letting sleep yank me down into the dark world I had been floating in since the world had filled with white light.

<hr>

MY EYES OPENED TO the canopy above my bed. Every muscle in my body felt as if someone had taken a training sword to it. I tried to move and groaned as new pains surfaced.

A chair scraped, and the bed squeaked.

I turned. Aiden sat on the edge of the bed. The dark circles under his eyes made me blink, and I raised my eyebrows.

"You look like hell," I whispered.

He smiled. "Well, at least one of us looks well rested." He glanced at the foot of the bed.

Shadow was curled up at my feet and sound asleep. I glanced back at Aiden. His smile faded.

"You scared the daylights out of me," he said and pushed the hair away from my face.

His touch sparked the same strong desire within me, and I leaned my cheek into his palm. His thumb traced my lips, and that deep longing surfaced in his eyes. He pulled his hand away and stood.

"I, um..." He closed his eyes. "I need to go. I just wanted to make sure you were all right before I left." He turned and started towards the door.

I forced myself into a sitting position. "No." The word came out strong.

His back stiffened and his hand hesitated on the doorknob, yet he didn't turn.

"Did that night mean nothing to you?"

He glanced over his shoulder at me, his eyes sad. "It meant everything to me."

Aiden slipped out the door, leaving me alone with my sleeping wolf pup and a body that felt like I had gone through a war. I climbed to my feet and nearly collapsed under a wave of dizziness. Sheer determination kept me moving, and I opened the door.

Aiden had his hands on the doorjamb and must have been resting his forehead against the wood. His head jerked back, and he stared down at me with wide eyes.

"Get back in bed." He straightened.

I held on to the door for support and shook my head. "Not unless you stay."

"I made a deal with your father, and now that you seem to be on the mend, I have to go."

"No more deals. No more threats. No more running. You are going to marry me."

He laughed, just as full and musical as I remembered. "Your parents will not buy into that, and I'd rather not have my head on the chopping block again."

"We lifted the curse, right?"

Aiden's gaze moved to my window and the bright light filtering in through the room. He nodded.

"So, what is the problem?"

"I damn near killed you." He glanced at my bandaged arm. He reached out to touch me, but he folded his fingers into a loose fist and took a step back.

"You were not in control."

He pressed his lips together in a tight line before sucking his lower lip into his mouth. "I might not have been in control, but I remember everything from the moment that thing took possession of you. And your arm isn't the only area I hurt."

"It wasn't you."

He glanced up at the ceiling. "It was, as much as I hate to admit it. That witch released my darkest desires while we were in the cave." His gaze dropped to mine.

I reached out and grabbed a fist full of his shirt, and his eyes widened when I yanked him in to the room. I stumbled, depleted of all my energy, and my weight slammed the door closed. My legs trembled, but I willed them to hold me in place. When I was sure I wouldn't crumple to the ground, I moved the wave of red hair that fell over my face and stared into his dazzling eyes.

"Please, don't go." I stepped towards him. My legs failed, but before I hit the ground, Aiden's strong arms caught me. He swept me up, carried me to the bed, and tucked me under the covers.

With a heavy sigh, he sat on the edge of the bed and took my hand. He turned it over and started the same slow inspection of my palm that I had done to him. His touch was soft and sensual. When his gaze finally rose to mine, a fire blazed in the blue depths.

"Do you want to be with me?" I whispered.

"I thought we established that pretty clearly in the cave."

"We established you wanted me. That is different."

A dimple appeared in his cheek, and he refocused on his inspection of my palm. The curve of his lips straightened as his fingers followed every line. His silence made my skin flush with uncertainty.

I tried to pull my hand away, but he gripped my wrist tighter, continuing his slow tracing of my palm.

"I can't imagine not being with you," he finally said. "But I am baffled that you still want to be with me with all that transpired." He let out a soft laugh. "Your father nearly beheaded me on the spot." His gaze lifted to mine. "I'm only alive because I had knowledge of blood transfusions."

My eyebrows knit together.

"I've studied at the monastery at night since I was old enough to read." He shrugged.

"Transfusion?" I asked, but my brain circled around the rest of his narrative.

He pointed to the bandage on the inside of my arm. "It saved your life."

I sat up, ignoring the wave of dizziness. "But..." Concern laced my voice as I glanced at the same bandage on the inside of his elbow.

He pressed his fingers to my lips. "The thing about blood... It regenerates over time as long as you don't lose too much. You lost way too much, so the only way to bring you back was to supplement your blood. I volunteered since I was the one who nearly drained you. That's why I look like hell, as you so eloquently put it."

"Oh." I blinked as some memories came rolling back. "I'm not sure what happened out there. I thought my father died, and then I saw him set a pig on fire?" I cocked my head, still fuzzy about what was fact and what had been conjured by my brain right before I had lost consciousness.

Aiden smiled. "Your father wielded a magic spell that fooled all of us, including Marigold. I couldn't believe he offered himself instead of you, and when it turned out to be a pig he was offering…" He chuckled and shook his head. "I didn't have a moment to appreciate that irony until now."

"She was a greedy witch," I said, remembering the intense interest that had sparked when she thought my father had offered himself in exchange for me. I shivered, and Aiden reached for my hand.

"Thank God for that." He squeezed my hand.

I couldn't agree more. "So, will you stay?"

"I made a deal with your father."

"You don't want to stay?" I slid my hand out from under his and crossed my arms. This deal stuff was bringing forth hot irritation, giving me the illusion of strength.

"I never said that." He leaned back, adopting the same posture.

The door opened, interrupting our standoff. My father walked in. Behind him, a servant carried a tray of food. It wasn't my lady-in-waiting, though.

"Where's Sheri?" I asked as the servant put the tray down on the table in the corner.

"I let her go," my father said and stared at Aiden.

Aiden lowered his eyes and gave a nod. He stood.

I grabbed his hand, refusing to let go, and glared at my father. "He is staying," I said, with a bite in my tone. "And I want Sheri back."

Tension layered the room. My father dismissed the servant with a wave. Once the door closed, his hard gaze bore into me.

Shadow lifted his head as if he knew there was another storm brewing.

My father opened his mouth.

"Father, I don't want to be disrespectful, but this is ridiculous. You pardoned the MacMahon name. The curse is lifted. So there is no reason for you to force Aiden to leave."

"After what he did to you?"

"He did nothing. Marigold made him do every slight you think he served me. And you vanquished her."

"I can speak for myself," Aiden said, glaring at me, squeezing my hand. "I had no control over what happened at

Stonehenge. The moment I met your daughter, I knew I would never willingly walk her into a death sentence. When I walked out of the throne room, I had already made peace with the fact I would be the last MacMahon to walk the earth, but your daughter sought me out." He dropped his gaze to mine. "And I made her angry," he finished, looking at my father. "I was the catalyst that let Marigold take possession."

My father's hands fisted, and his eyes flashed cold.

"He made me angry because he refused me." I didn't want to fuel whatever fury had been building in my father by telling him we had slept together and then he had refused me. He would never understand that. But he needed to know exactly why I got angry. Otherwise, his mind would go where it didn't belong.

His hands uncurled, and his brow furrowed. "You... refused her?"

I squeezed Aiden's hand in a silent warning.

"Aye. I love your daughter, and I could not sentence her to a cursed life."

My entire body froze at his admission, and I stared up at Aiden with a slack jaw. A smirk cracked my father's face. He tried to wipe it off before I saw it, but he wasn't fast enough. I snapped my mouth closed.

He studied Aiden with a deep crevice on his brow.

Aiden shifted and dropped his gaze to the floor.

My father slowly crossed his arms. "Let's say I entertained my daughter's insane idea. What do you have to offer in exchange for her hand?"

My skin tingled with shock, and my eyes widened.

"I wouldn't barter for her like she is livestock," Aiden sneered.

"Is that because you have nothing to give?"

"No. It's because she is a beautiful woman who should be treated as an equal. A partner. You don't barter for a heart like it is a thing to be collected or owned." There was just enough distaste in his voice for my father's eyes to narrow.

My heart soared.

"However, if you were to give this union your blessing, I would promise to love her until my dying breath. To make sure her life was filled with joy and to do my best to protect her from the sorrows in this world." He glanced at me and then back at my father.

"And marrying her would give you the throne," he said, his face still pinched with distrust.

"No, Your Majesty. When the time comes, May will rule. And I will follow my queen to the ends of the earth if that is what is required."

My father's eyebrows arched, and his mouth popped open for the briefest of instances. He glanced at our clasped hands and stroked his beard thoughtfully. "I still do not trust your motives, Mr. MacMahon. However, your argument is compelling enough to give you and my daughter some time to court. If, after a fortnight, she still wants to marry you, I will consider it." He turned and started towards the door, but paused before he left the room. "And that does not mean screwing her, you understand?" He glared over his shoulder.

Aiden nodded, and my father strolled out.

I blinked, staring after him, and then my gaze snapped to Aiden's. He stared at the door, dumbstruck, with his jaw hanging open. When his gaze slid to mine, it held something I hadn't ever seen in his eyes. Hope.

# BRAVE Chapter 11

AIDEN HELD MY HAND as we walked through the woods. The electricity between the two of us had only grown since my father gave us his permission to court. But this was the first time we'd had the strength to leave the castle grounds. Shadow bounded ahead, pouncing on rustling leaves and generally being a puppy.

I smiled at the wolf's enthusiasm, as well as his need to keep returning to us to make sure we were still nearby.

The past week had been filled with conversation and chess matches, while we both recuperated from Marigold's aftermath. We saw eye to eye on many things, but my father's rule was not one of them. That had been the source of many quiet but spirited debates. He had hardly touched me since my father made our courting rules clear, and it was driving me mad.

Aiden's easy smile warmed my insides, and all I could think about were his arms around me and his mouth on mine.

"Do you want to go to the cave?" I asked, afraid to look at him.

His gait slowed. "Why?" he asked, his voice cautious.

I glanced at him. "I'd like my hunting clothes back," I said, batting my eyelashes.

He chuckled. "Liar."

Heat filled my cheeks, and I suppressed a smile. Instead of

dignifying his accurate assessment, I kept walking.

"If we go, will you behave?"

I grinned and looked at the ground, letting my loose hair hide my face. He swept it away and stared at me with a cocked eyebrow.

I rolled my eyes. "Aye, I'll behave."

He kicked at the leaves and sighed. "Sure."

We kept to the woods instead of crossing through Stonehenge, and it took us longer to get to the cave entrance than it would have if we had crossed through the great rocks. Navigating in the darkness proved to be more challenging than either Aiden or I thought it would be. Without the benefit of the bear curse, Aiden was just as blind as I was. Every time he stumbled, foul language tumbled out of his lips and I would giggle. By the time we entered the cavern, his face was red with frustration. I crossed to my crumpled pile of clothes and folded them neatly on the rock.

The splash of water pulled me away from my task, and I turned. Aiden's clothing was piled on the shore, and his bare ass broke the surface as he crossed the expanse beyond the cold current into the hot springs on the other side. He stood in waist-deep water with his back to me and wiped his hair off his face before turning in my direction.

Aiden looked tired, but more refreshed than he had all week.

"What happened to behave?" I asked.

He just grinned. "I'm behaving."

I cocked my eyebrow.

"What? A man can't take a swim?"

I kicked my boots off and stripped. Aiden's gaze traveled from head to toe and back before I dived into the water. When I surfaced, I understood his sudden burst of energy. The water was invigorating until I swam into the cold spot. The river's current pulled at me, and I didn't have the strength to fight it. My eyes widened in fear as I was sucked down under the surface.

Aiden moved fast, grabbing my hand. He yanked me to the surface and into his powerful arms, leading me to the hot springs beyond the frigid underground river. With his arms wrapped around me, I laid my cheek against his chest, trying to catch my breath. His heart beat just as wildly as mine.

"Maybe this wasn't such a good idea," he said once his breathing slowed.

I stayed in place, enjoying being in his grasp. He kissed the top of my head and stroked the hair away from my face. With his palms resting on my cheekbones, and his fingers threaded into my hair, he studied my face with such seriousness, I almost squirmed.

He leaned in and gently captured my lips in the sweetest kiss. Warmth spread from my core all the way to my fingers and toes, rivaling the hot springs surrounding me.

My fingers glided down his chiseled chest to the outline of his hips. I opened my mouth, and our tongues rolled together in a seductive dance. When my hand wrapped around his manhood, he gasped and pulled away from my lips. His body remained in place.

"May, I promised your father."

I gently stroked him and smiled. "You promised you wouldn't screw me. I don't see us screwing, do you?"

He blinked and then closed his eyes, letting out a groan. "No, but if you continue what you're doing, I'll lose any sort of restraint I have," he said, but didn't stop the slow movement of my hands.

His jaw tightened, and the veins in his neck stood out as he looked down at me. Hunger invaded his features, and it thrilled me. This was the same look he had when he'd taken me that first time. His lips crushed mine, and he turned me into the rocks. His mouth was greedy and insistent, and his tongue explored the depths of my mouth.

He still tasted like honey. My knees weakened at the power in the kiss. I stroked faster, and he groaned into my mouth. His hands lay flat on the rock on either side of my head, as if touching me would melt all his resolve. Just our lips and my hands remained in contact.

"Stop," he whispered against my lips. "Please. I won't have enough energy to get us across the river if you don't." He opened his eyes and met my gaze. Raw need blazed in his irises.

As much as I wanted to satisfy the need in both of us, I pulled my hands away, leaving us both frustrated and on edge. It was a sound strategy, especially since we struggled with the river's undercurrent as we headed back to the shore.

The moment we stepped onto the sand, Aiden pulled me into a bear hug. His lips found the spot where my neck and shoulder met, sending gooseflesh across my skin. He held me tight while his hardness pressed into my stomach with nothing to stop him from lifting me in his arms and taking me right there, but he restrained.

He released me and stepped away. His chest rose and fell like he had sprinted to the castle and back, mimicking mine. I stepped close and dropped to my knees. His eyes widened, and the moment my mouth slipped over the tip of his member, a low moan escaped his lips.

His fingers threaded into my hair as he guided me. His grip tightened, and I met his gaze. He stepped back, away from me, his entire body trembling. I stayed on my knees, wiping my mouth with the back of my hand.

His chin dipped to his chest, and his fists clenched as tight as his eyes. He took deep breaths, and when his eyelids flew open, I knew he'd lost the battle.

He pushed me back in the sand, and I wrapped my legs around his waist. This time, he slid inside me with care, his eyes rolling back as he went.

I winced when his entire length filled me, and he stilled, searching my eyes. I was still sore from what Marigold had made him do to me, but I wanted this. I wanted him.

"My god, you are heaven," he whispered, and kissed me again, remaining still until I ground my hips to his. He moved slowly, savoring the burn, and I focused on the tingling pleasure every time our hips met.

This was the opposite of our frantic first time; it was sweet and gentle and made me forget about the aching soreness. By the time he was ready, so was I, and our cadence sped up until we both cried out, our names echoing in the chamber.

He rolled off me and stared at the ceiling. "Your father is going to kill me," he said and covered his face.

I glanced over at him. "It's not like you could have told him we didn't sleep together before this," I said, flashing a smile.

"True." He lowered his arms and took my hand in his, his gaze on the ceiling. "You still want to marry me after a week in my company?"

"Only if you want to still marry me."

He turned his head, and the most glorious smile spread across his lips. "I could spend a hundred lifetimes with you, and it still wouldn't be enough." He climbed to his feet. "We should head back."

Before getting dressed, we washed the sand off each other. Aiden gathered what little belongings he had. It all fit in a satchel he had stowed in the corner, and he slung it over his shoulder.

I hand combed my wet locks and scooped up my hunting clothes before we headed out the way we had come. This time, we were both more surefooted, and we stepped out of the woods to a stunning sunset.

"I don't know about you, but I don't think I have enough energy to go around this time," Aiden said as Shadow danced around our feet.

I stared at Stonehenge. A dark shiver ran down my spine. The shortest route was right through the thing, but I did not want to step inside the rocks. "As long as we go around the rocks to the south, I'm fine."

He nodded, understanding. The north side was where my father had beaten Marigold, and going near where she was killed felt too much like tempting fate.

<hr>

EVERY MUSCLE FELT LIKE putty by the time we got to the castle. Aiden looked every bit as exhausted as I felt. The only one of us that seemed to exude energy was Shadow.

My stomach growled loud enough for Aiden to glance at me.

"I could eat an entire deer right now," he said.

"You and me both."

"Where have you been?"

My mother's voice cut through the courtyard, making me jump.

We both turned towards her.

"We went to pick up my things," Aiden said. "It took us longer than expected. I'm sorry if we worried you, my lady," he said with a sweeping bow. He stood and gave her a crooked smile of apology.

She wrung her hands together, and her gaze bounced between us. "There is still food in the dining hall." She waved towards the great hall. "Your father has been waiting for your return."

I blinked the exhaustion away and handed my clothes to the nearest servant. We followed my mother into the dining hall to get some much-needed food.

My father sat at the center of the table with his arms crossed and only a wineglass in front of him. Most of the food had been removed, but it looked like a meat pie and some fruits remained.

I crossed to the food. Aiden followed me, and we piled our plates high with whatever was left. When we were done serving ourselves, there were only crumbs left on the serving platters.

I nearly fell into the closest seat. Aiden collapsed next to me. I was too tired and hungry to mind my manners, and I stuffed a large piece of meat into my mouth just as my father spoke.

"Where have you been?"

Aiden also had a mouthful, so I put my finger up, asking for another minute before answering.

"They went to get Aiden's belongings," my mother said for me.

I nodded, still chewing.

My father sipped his wine, studying us as we ate. I knew I was eating at a speed that wasn't normal, and when I finished everything on my plate, I leaned back and belched.

"Sorry, but the walk took every ounce of energy from both of us," I said as I wiped my lips.

Aiden showed more restraint, finishing a few minutes after I did, and he sat back in the chair, closing his eyes. "Thank you for the delicious meal," he said, like he had each night he'd joined us for dinner.

"Tomorrow, we hunt," my father said.

Aiden opened his eyes and stared at him. "You want me to hunt with you?"

"Yes. I want to see how good you are with a bow and arrow."

I studied my father, gauging whether this was some sort of trap. "What are you hunting?"

"It seems there has been another bear sighting." My father glared at me for a moment before refocusing on Aiden.

Aiden's smile faded. "An arrow is just going to piss a bear off."

"Then you better have good aim."

"I have impeccable aim, but a bear's hide is thick. The only time an arrow is successful is from close proximity." Aiden shifted in his seat and glanced at me. "I'm not sure I'm in the most optimal health to take on a bear." His cheeks turned red.

"Father," I started, but he raised his hand.

"No arguments. He is going, or he is leaving this province for good," he said.

I balked.

"I would be honored, Your Highness," Aiden said.

Even though Aiden's answer lacked sincerity, my father nodded and raised his glass. "To success."

Aiden and I raised our glasses as well.

"Aiden will stay in my room tonight," I said.

My father spit his wine out. Aiden choked on his wine, coughing and sputtering as he looked at me with wide eyes. My mother's jaw hung open.

"Over my dead body," my father answered and wiped his chin.

"If you insist on bringing him on this fool's errand, I would at least like to know what it feels like to lie in his arms." I tilted my head as if I had just asked for honey in my tea instead of calling my father out on his outrageous idea.

"May," Aiden wheezed. "Please don't make a scene. I will be fine." He tried to take my hand.

I yanked it away from him. "We barely survived today's walk without collapsing. How are you going to be sharp enough to kill a bear?" I glared at him. "The last time you went up against a full-grown grizzly, you were a bear, and you were almost killed. Am I supposed to smile and wave good luck to you when I know you are walking into a death trap?" I spun on my father. "And you, you were almost annihilated by that bear, too. How do you expect to survive with someone so weak at your side?"

My father placed his cup on the table and met my glare.

"I am not weak," Aiden said from behind me, his voice full of steel and fire.

I turned to him and put my hand on top of his clenched fist. "Normally, you are not. But you are still recovering from the transfusion. You were the one who told me it would take a couple of months before either of us was at full strength. And you need to be at full strength to go after a bear."

My father crossed his arms and leaned back in the chair while my mother busied herself by smoothing out the folds of her dress.

I glanced at all three of them. Neither my father nor Aiden budged in their commitment.

"Well, then, if you go, I go," I said.

Both Aiden's and my father's expressions mirrored each other's. The first thing to fade was the anger, and then their eyes widened. Before either of them spoke, their heads shook. As one, they said, "No."

"You will stay in bed and rest," Aiden said. "And I will not be joining you in your room tonight, regardless of what you want. This is your father's house. His roof, his rules."

"Then it is settled," my father said and stood, taking his leave with my mother.

"Aiden." I turned to him.

He pressed his fingers to my lips. "Stop. I promise I will be fine." He leaned close and gave me a light kiss. "I will see you tomorrow when I return from the hunt."

I watched him go with my stomach in knots.

# BRAVE Chapter 12

SUNLIGHT STREAMED THROUGH MY window. I blinked, disoriented. I didn't think sleep would ever come, but it had and deep enough for me to miss seeing the hunt off.

The shuffle of fabric made me jump. I snapped my head to my dressing table. My mother sat in the seat watching me with a hint of a smile on her face.

She stood, crossed to the bed, and took a seat on the edge. "Your father will make sure nothing happens to Aiden. He actually has grown fond of him, but needs to test where his loyalties lie."

"By going after a bear?" I said and sat up. A deep ache in my muscles reminded me of our activities yesterday.

"No, by protecting his king."

I cocked my head.

"I don't understand it either. I told him it was foolish, but they won't be the only ones out there. Samuel and Edward are going with them."

I relaxed a fraction. Both Samuel and Edward were accomplished with a bow and arrow, as well as a sword. They had to be as my father's closest guards. But the gnawing worry persisted in my belly.

I slipped out of bed, wincing at the tightness in my derriere. I limped to my wardrobe and pulled out a proper dress for the day. What I really wanted to do was put my hunting clothing on and go after him, but I knew Aiden would be aggravated with me. Besides, how far would I really get with the state of my body?

After I dressed, my mother brushed my hair, and I closed my eyes, taken back to when I was little and she would spend hours brushing my hair until it had shone in the candlelight. Her soft touch relaxed me. When she set the brush down, I met her gaze.

"Your father sees how happy this man makes you and wants to be sure his motives are pure."

"Aiden's motives *are* pure."

Her smile seemed strained, but she nodded and helped me down to the sitting room to wait for the men to arrive home. I paced while she patiently sewed.

Finally, she put her embroidery on the table. "May, sit down. You are making me just as jumpy as you are."

The sun had passed beyond midday, and while I knew the men wouldn't be back until dusk, I still had an unsettledness that I couldn't calm.

"I can't. Not until Aiden is back safe."

My mother shifted and glanced out the window. The worry lines around her mouth grew deeper, and she shook her head, replacing them with a smile instead. But the glimpse of her unease was enough for me to take a seat and still my restlessness.

Moments later, commotion filled the castle, followed by the shattering of stoneware. My mother and I both stood and ran toward the great hall. I stopped at the door, trying to reconcile what I was seeing. The dishes and candles for the feast had been carelessly swept from the table, and my father lay on the wood plank with his leg drenched with blood.

Aiden's shirt was streaked red.

My heart plummeted.

Aiden turned in my direction. "Get bandages and wine now!"

My feet wouldn't move. The side of his face bled from claw marks, but he didn't seem to notice. My mother disappeared from my side.

Aiden looked at Samuel on the other side of the table. "Go put the blade of your sword in the kitchen kiln until the handle is almost too hot to hold and then bring it back."

Samuel limped away, leaving Aiden alone with Edward and my father.

"You will need to hold him still when Samuel comes back, understand?" Aiden barked at Edward.

Edward nodded.

Aiden tore the splint off my father's leg and tossed it aside. He ripped the wet fabric of my father's pant leg.

I gasped. My father's eyes dulled enough to jumpstart my heart and I raced to his side.

"What happened?" I asked.

"Your betrothed saved my life," my father said, his voice laced with agony.

"I haven't saved you yet," Aiden said, tightening a belt around my father's thigh.

His lower leg looked like the bear had used it as a scratching post. His skin was torn to the bone, and the bone poked out of the skin.

Samuel came back in the room with his sword glowing red, and my mother came in with an armful of bandages.

"Move his good leg," Aiden said and took the sword from Samuel. "And give him something to bite down on."

"What are you doing?" My father's eyes widened, making his features much paler.

Aiden glanced at him. "Your leg or your life. That's the choice."

"Just bandage it up," my father insisted.

Aiden glanced at Edward. "Put your belt in his mouth," he said.

Edward slid his belt off, doubled it, and shoved it between my father's teeth. Then he pulled my father's good leg far enough away to not get hit with the glowing blade in Aiden's hands.

He lined up the blade and looked at my mother.

"Don't you dare," my father growled around the leather.

"He won't make it," Aiden said softly.

My mother nodded. "Take his leg," she ordered.

Without hesitation, Aiden brought the sword down, yelling with the force of it. Skin sizzled. The blade embedded in the wood below my father's leg.

My father screamed despite still clamping down on the belt.

Aiden turned to me. "Get me honey."

I turned and ran into the kitchen. When I came back, Aiden was sewing a patch of skin he had ripped from my father's discarded appendage onto the blunt end of my father's leg while my mother poured wine over the wound. My father had already passed out.

As soon as he was done stitching skin to skin, he dried the leg with the bandage and threw it on the floor. Then he turned to me with his hand out.

"Honey," he said, and this time his voice sounded a little weaker.

I poured it into his hand, and he slathered it on the wound before wrapping my father's leg.

When he finished, he wiped his hands and took a seat. "You can take him up to his bed. We will need to change that daily until it heals," he said to my mother.

She nodded. Edward and Samuel helped carry my father as my mother led the way.

I picked up a clean bandage and doused it with wine. Stepping closer to Aiden, I tilted his chin up so I could see his wounds better. I dabbed the cuts. He didn't even wince. Instead, he gave me a tired smile.

"I couldn't get to him before the bear did." He brought his hand to his face. When he pulled his fingers away, wine and blood covered them. "But I took that bastard down." He stared at his hand. "How bad is it?"

"Not bad," I said and smoothed a thin layer of honey over the cuts. None of them were deep enough for me to stitch, but they would leave a scar. I glanced at the table and the wood still smoking from the hot sword. "Where did you learn that?"

"Same place I learned about transfusions," he said and wiped his face.

"Come on. Let's get you cleaned up." I helped him to his feet and let him use me for support.

Now that his adrenaline had faded, his steps were unsteady. I took him to the bathing area and stripped him of the soiled clothing, inspecting every inch of him to make sure there weren't any more wounds. After my thorough once-over, I helped him into the iron tub.

"It isn't the hot springs." I handed him a washcloth and poured warm pots of water over him until the water ran clear down his chest.

He scrubbed his hands as I cleaned his hair and shoulders with a second cloth. When he was done, he leaned back in the tub and just stared at me.

"Did your father say betrothed?" he asked, his sleepy eyes searching mine.

"Yes."

Aiden smiled and climbed to his feet, drying off with a towel I handed him. The wardrobe in the bath had a few extra pairs of clothes, and I handed some to him. I didn't think my father would mind.

Aiden pulled on the clothes, and then I led him to my room and made him sit at my vanity while I spread another thin layer of honey on the cuts. Then, I made him lie down under the covers in my bed. Before I finished tucking him in, he had fallen asleep.

Instead of climbing in with him like every fiber of me wanted to, I went to my parents' room and stepped inside. My father lay under the covers and my mother gently swiped his forehead with a cloth. She looked up at me; her smile tense.

"Thank Aiden for me," she said. "If your father pulls through this fever, he won't be happy with the choice I made, but he will adjust." She wiped his forehead again.

"If?" I blinked and stared at my father, looking so meek and sickly in the bed.

My mother raised her gaze and nodded.

I came to her side and reached for my father's hand. "Father, please fight this. I want you to walk me down the aisle. I want you there to celebrate and drink wine until you say something incredibly sappy and sweet. I need you to be there, so please fight this fever and come back to Mother and me." I squeezed his hand and kissed his cheek before I gave my mother a hug. While I wanted to stay and carry on the vigil with her, I knew she wanted this time with my father.

"Let me know if anything changes," I said and headed back to my room. I stripped my clothing and pulled on a nightshirt, climbed under the covers, and snuggled next to Aiden.

He rolled, wrapping his arms around me, and pulled me tight to his chest. The cadence of his breathing smoothed out again.

With his arms around me, he soothed all my worries about what was to come. I didn't know if tonight would change my father's acceptance of Aiden, or if he would default to exiling him out of anger for his own situation.

I could only pray that all would work out. Just before I drifted to sleep, I caught Aiden's soft whisper of my name. Calm settled over me. If there was a fight to be had, we would hit it head-on.

I smiled and let the night pull me into its depths.

# BRAVE Chapter 13

TOWN BELLS RANG, AND the doors to the throne room opened. Anyone who was anybody stood within the walls. The place was packed beyond capacity. I marveled at the town's finery on display.

After all, a royal wedding was at hand.

A thin aisle separated the rows of chairs on the main floor, and as the crowd turned to face us, Aiden stepped into view.

My heart stilled, and I sighed at his regal beauty.

He looked magnificent in the formal clothing of the court. His tunic was a deep blue with black leather insets that matched his pants and boots. His crest stood out against the crushed velvet, adding to his outfit. He clasped his hands behind his back and turned fully in my direction. The minute our eyes met, an electrical current passed between us as strong as it had that first night we had met.

Aiden's smile grew into a magnificent grin that brightened my heart. I could see the twinkle in his eyes, even at this distance.

"Are you sure about this man?" my father asked, leaning into me as if what he had said was a big secret.

I glanced at him with his crutch under one arm and his other hooked through mine. "I've never been surer of anything in my life."

With that, we started the slow procession towards a future filled with promise and adventure, not to mention all the steam I could handle.

## The End

If you enjoyed BRAVE: A FRACTURED FAIRY TALE, please consider leaving a review!

Find more books by J.E. Taylor on her website: http://books.jetaylor75.com/

# About J.E. Taylor

J.E. Taylor is a USA Today bestselling author, a publisher, an editor, a manuscript formatter, a mother, a wife, a business analyst, and a Supernatural fangirl. Not necessarily in that order. She first sat down to seriously write in February of 2007 after her daughter asked:

"Mom, if you could do anything, what would you do?"
From that moment on, she hasn't looked back.

Besides being co-owner of Novel Concept Publishing, Ms. Taylor also moonlights as a Senior Editor of Allegory (www.allegoryezine.com), an online venue for Science Fiction, Fantasy and Horror. J.E. Taylor is also one of the co-hosts of the popular podcast Spilling Ink.

She lives in New Hampshire with her husband and two children and during the summer months enjoys her weekends on the shore in southern Maine.

Visit her at www.books.jetaylor75.com and sign up for her newsletter for early previews of her upcoming books!

If you liked BRAVE, you might also like these other fairy tales and magical romance stories from J.E. Taylor's backlist:

# A FRACTURED FAIRY TALE

# BOOKS 1-10

Little Red Riding Hood, Cinderella, Brave, Rapunzel, Frozen, Snow White, Sleeping Beauty, Aladdin, Beauty and the Beast and Peter Pan – all fairy tales you know and love, but twisted, fractured into something new.

Shifters and magic claw through the pages of these fractured fairy tales, giving you a thrilling take on an old tale.

Will the heroine survive whatever the evil villain has in store?  Or will Love conquer all?

Grab your hardcover edition of A Fractured Fairy Tale – books 1-10 and find out!

A Fractured Fairy Tale books 1-10 includes

Red, Cinder, Brave, Tangled, Frozen, Snow, Spindle, Jasmine, Belle, Hook

Find these titles and other fantasy and suspense titles on J.E. Taylor's website!

https://JETaylor75.com

www.ingramcontent.com/pod-product-compliance
Lightning Source LLC
Chambersburg PA
CBHW031132130726
47988CB00006B/2335